Philip Doddridge

Some Remarkable Passages in the Life of the Honourable Col. James

Gardiner

Who was slain at the battle of Preston Pans, September 21, 1745

Philip Doddridge

Some Remarkable Passages in the Life of the Honourable Col. James Gardiner
Who was slain at the battle of Preston Pans, September 21, 1745

ISBN/EAN: 9783337213800

Printed in Europe, USA, Canada, Australia, Japan

Cover: Foto ©Raphael Reischuk / pixelio.de

More available books at **www.hansebooks.com**

SOME

REMARKABLE PASSAGES

IN THE

L I F E

OF THE HONOURABLE

COL. JAMES GARDINER,

Who was flain at the Battle of PRESTON-PANS, *September* 21, 1745.

TO WHICH IS ADDED,

THE SERMON

Occafioned by his HEROIC DEATH.

BY P. DODDRIDGE, D. D.

—————— *Juftior alter*
Nec Pietate fuit, nec Bello major & Armis.   VIRG.

PHILADELPHIA:

PRINTED AND SOLD BY STEWART & COCHRAN,
N°. 34, SOUTH SECOND-STREET.

M, DCC, XCV.

DAVID GARDINER, Esq.

Cornet in Sir John Cope's

Regiment of Dragoons.

DEAR SIR,

WHILE my heart is following you with a truly pater-nal folicitude, through all the dangers of military life, in which you are thus early engaged, anxious for your fafety amidſt the inſtruments of death, and the far more dangerous allurements of vice ; I feel a peculiar pleaſure in being able. at length, though after ſuch long delays, to put into your hands the MEMOIRS with which I now preſent you. They contain many particulars, which would have been worthy of your attentive notice, had they related to a perfon of the moſt diſtant nation or age : But they will, I doubt not, command your peculiar regard, as they are ſacred to the memory of that excellent man, from whom you had the honour to derive your birth, and by whoſe generous and affectionate care, you have been laid under all the obliga-tions, which the beſt of fathers could confer on a moſt be-loved ſon.

Here, Sir, you ſee a gentleman, who with all the advan-tages of a liberal and religious education, added to every na-tural accompliſhment that could render him moſt agreeable, entered, before he had attained the ſtature of a man, on thoſe arduous and generous ſervices to which you are devoted, and behaved in them with a gallantry and courage, which will always give a ſplendor to his name among the Britiſh ſoldiery, and render him an example to all officers of his rank. But alas ! amidſt all the intrepidity of the Martial Hero, you ſee him vanquiſhed by the blandiſhments of pleasure, and in chace of it plunging himself into follies and vices, for which no want of education or genius could have been a sufficient excuse. You behold him urging the ignoble and fatal pursuit, unmoved by the terrors which death was continually darting around him, and the most signal deliverances by which Providence again and again rescued him from those terrors; till at length he was reclaimed by an ever-memorable interposition of divine grace. Then you have the pleasure of seeing him become in good earnest a convert to Christianity, and by speedy advances growing up into one of its brightest ornaments; his mind continually filled with the great ideas which the gospel of our Redeemer suggests, and bringing the blessed influence of its sublime principles into every relation of military and civil, of public and domestic life. You trace him persevering in a steady and uniform course of goodness, through a long series of honourable and prosperous years, the delight of all that were so happy as to know him, and, in his sphere, the most faithful guardian of his country ; till at last, worn out with honourable labours, and broken with infirmities which they had hastened upon him before the time, you see him forgetting them at once at the call of duty and Providence ; with all the generous ardour of his most vigorous days rushing on the enemies of religion and liberty, sustaining their shock with the most deliberate fortitude, when deserted by those that should have supported him, and chearfully sacrificing the little remains of a mortal life, in the triumphant views of a glorious immortality.

This, Sir, is the noble object I present to your view ; and you will, I hope, fix your eye continually upon it, and will never allow yourself for one day to forget, that this illustrious man is COLONEL GARDINER, your ever honoured father ; who having approved his *fidelity to the death* and received *a crown of life*, seems as it were, by what you here read, to be calling out to you from amidst *the cloud of witnesses* with which you are surrounded, and urging you by every generous, tender, filial sentiment, to mark the footsteps of his Christian race, and strenuously to maintain that combat, where the victory is through divine grace certain, and the prize an eternal kingdom in the heavens.

My hopes, Sir, that all thefe powerful motives will efpe-cially have their full efficacy on you, are greatly encouraged by the certainty which I have of your being well acquainted with the evidence of Chriftianity in its full extent; a cri-minal ignorance of which, in the midft of great advantages for learning them, leaves fo many of our young people a prey to Deifm, and fo to vice and ruin, which generally bring up its rear. My life would be a continual burthen to me, if I had not a confcioufnefs in the fight of God, that during the years in which the important truft of your education was committed to my care, I had laid before you the proofs both of natural and revealed religion, in what I affuredly efteem to be, with regard to the judgment, if they are carefully ex-amined, an irrefiftable light; and that I had endeavoured to attend them with thofe addreffes, which might be moft likely to imprefs your heart. You have not, dear Sir, forgotten, and I am confident you can never entirely forget, the affi-duity with which I have laboured to form your mind, not only to what might be ornamental to you in human life, but above all to a true tafte of what is really excellent, and an early contempt of thofe vanities by which the generality of our youth, efpecially in your ftation, are debafed, enervated, and undone. My private as well as public addreffes for this purpofe will, I know, be remembered by you, and the tears of tendernefs with which they have fo often been ac-companied: And may they be fo remembered, that they who are moft tenderly concerned, may be comforted under the lofs of fuch an ineftimable friend as Colonel Gardiner, by feeing that his character, in all its moft amiable and re-fplendent parts, lives in you; and that how difficult foever it may be to act up to that height of expectation, with which the eyes of the world will be fixed on the fon of fuch a fa-ther, you are, in the ftrength of divine grace attempting it; at leaft are following him with generous emulation, and with daily folicitude, that the fteps may be lefs unequal!

May the Lord God of your father, and I will add, of both your pious and honourable parents, animate your heart more and more with fuch views and fentiments as thefe! May he guard your life amidft every fcene of danger, to be

a protection and bleffing to thofe that are yet unborn; and
may He give you, in fome far diftant period of time, to refign it by a gentler diffolution than the hero from whom
you fprung; or if unerring wifdom appoint otherwife, to
end it with equal glory.

I am,

Dear Sir,

Your ever faithful,

Affectionate Friend, and

Obliged humble fervant,

P. DODDRIDGE.

NORTHAMPTON, ⎱
  July 1, 1747. ⎰

SOME
REMARKABLE PASSAGES

IN THE

L I F E

OF THE HONOURABLE

Col. JAMES GARDINER.

§ 1. WHEN I promifed the public fome larger account of the life and character of this illuftrious perfon, than I could conveniently infert in my fermon on the fad occafion of his death, I was fecure, that, if providence continued my capacity of writing, I fhould not wholly difappoint the expectation. For I was furnifhed with a variety of particulars, which appeared to me worthy of general notice, in confequence of that intimate friendfhip with which he had honoured me during the fix laft years of his life; a friend-fhip which led him to open his heart to me in repeated con-verfations with an unbounded confidence, (as he then affur-ed me, beyond what he had ufed with any other man liv-ing,) fo far as religious experiences were concerned: And I had alfo received feveral very valuable letters from him, during the time of our abfence from each other, which con-tained moft genuine and edifying traces of his chriftian cha-racter. But I hoped farther to learn many valuable particulars from the papers of his own clofet; and from his letters to other friends, as well as from what they more circumftan-tially knew concerning him: I therefore determined to de-lay the execution of my promife, till I could enjoy thefe advantages for performing it in the moſt ſatisfactory manner; nor have I, on the whole, reaſon to regret that determination.

§. 2. I ſhall not trouble my reader with all the cauſes, which concurred to retard theſe expected aſſiſtances for almoſt a whole year: The chief of them were, the tedious languiſhing illneſs of his afflicted lady, through whoſe hands it was proper the papers ſhould paſs; together with the confuſion into which the rebels had thrown them, when they ranſacked his ſeat at Bankton, where moſt of them were depoſited. But having now received ſuch of them, as have eſcaped their rapacious hands, and could conveniently be collected and tranſmitted, I ſet myſelf with the greateſt pleaſure to perform, what I eſteem, not merely a tribute of gratitude to the memory of my invaluable friend, (though never was the memory of any mortal man more precious and ſacred to me;) but of duty to God, and my fellow-creatures: For I have a moſt chearful hope, that the narrative I am now to write will, under the divine bleſſing, be a means of ſpreading, what of all things in the world every benevolent heart will moſt deſire to ſpread, a warm and lively ſenſe of religion.

§. 3. My own heart has been ſo much edified and animated, by what I have read in the memoirs of perſons who have been eminent for wiſdom and piety, that I cannot but wiſh the treaſure may be more and more increaſed: And I would hope, the world may gather the like valuable fruits from the life I am now attempting; not only as it will contain very ſingular circumſtances, which may excite a general curioſity, but as it comes attended with ſome other particular advantages.

§. 4. The reader is here to ſurvey a character of ſuch eminent and various goodneſs, as might demand veneration, and inſpire him with a deſire to imitate it too, had it appeared in the obſcureſt rank: But it will ſurely command ſome peculiar regard. when viewed in ſo elevated and important a ſtation; eſpecially as it ſhone, not in eccleſiaſtical, but military life, where the temptations are ſo many, and the prevalency of the contrary character ſo great, that it may ſeem no inconſiderable praiſe and felicity to be free from diſſolute vice, and to retain what in moſt other profeſſions might be eſteemed only a mediocrity of virtue. It may ſurely with the higheſt juſtice be expected, that the title and bravery of Colonel Gardiner will invite many of our officers and ſoldiers, to whom his name has long been honourable and dear, to peruſe this account of him with ſome peculiar attention : In conſequence of which, it may be a means of increaſing the number, and brightening the character, of thoſe who are already adorning their office, their country, and their religion ; and of reclaiming thoſe, who will ſee rather what they ought to be, than what they are. On the whole, to the *gentlemen of the ſword* I would particularly offer theſe memoirs, as theirs by ſo diſtinguiſhed a title : Yet I am firmly perſuaded, there are none, whoſe office is ſo ſacred, or whoſe proficiency in the religious life is ſo advanced, but they may find ſomething to demand their thankfulneſs, and to awaken their emulation.

§. 5. Colonel James Gardiner, of whom we write, was the ſon of Captain Patrick Gardiner, of the family of Torwood-Head, by Mrs. Mary Hodge, of the family of Gladſmuir. The Captain who was maſter of a handſome eſtate, ſerved many years in the army of King William and Queen Anne, and died abroad with the Britiſh forces in Germany, quickly after the battle of Hochſtet, through the fatigues he underwent in the duties of that celebrated campaign. He had a company in the regiment of foot, once commanded by Colonel Hodge, his valiant brother-in-law, who was ſlain at the head of that regiment, (my memorial from Scotland ſays,) at the battle of Steenkirk, which was fought in the year 1692.

§ 6. Mrs. Gardner, our Colonel's mother, was a lady of a very valuable character ; but it pleaſed God to exerciſe her with very uncommon trials : For ſhe not only loſt her huſband and her brother in the ſervice of their country, as before related, but alſo her eldeſt ſon, Mr. Robert Gardiner, on the day which compleated the 16th year of his age, at the ſiege of Namur, in 1695. But there is great reaſon to believe, God bleſſed theſe various and heavy afflictions, as the means of forming her to that eminent degree of piety, which will render her memory honourable as long as it continues.

§. 7. Her ſecond ſon, the worthy perſon of whom I am now to give a more particular account, was born at Carriden, in Linlithgow-ſhire, on the 10th of January, A. D.

1687-8 ; the memorable year of that glorious revolution which he juſtly eſteemed among the happieſt of all events. So that when he was ſlain in the defence of thoſe liberties, which God then by ſo gracious a providence reſcued from utter deſtruction, *i. e,* on the 21ſt of September, 1745, he was aged 57 years, 8 months, and 14 days.

§. 8. The annual return of his birth day was obſerved by him, in the latter and better years of his life, in a manner very different from what is commonly practiſed : For inſtead of making it a day of feſtivity, I am told, he rather diſtinguiſhed it as a ſeaſon of more than ordinary humiliation before God ; both in commemoration of thoſe mercies which he received in the firſt opening of life, and under an affectionate ſenſe, as well of his long alienation from the great author and ſupport of his being, as of the many imperfections which he lamented, in the beſt of his days and ſervices.

§. 9. I have not met with many things remarkable concerning the early years of his life, only that his mother took care to inſtruct him with great tenderneſs and affection, in the principles of true chriſtianity. He was alſo trained up in human literature at the ſchool at Linlithgow, where he made a very conſiderable progreſs in the languages. I remember to have heard him quote ſome paſſages of the Latin Claſſicks very pertinently ; though his employment in life, and the various turns which his mind took under different impulſes in ſucceeding years, prevented him from cultivating ſuch ſtudies.

§. 10. The good effects of his mother's prudent and exemplary care were not ſo conſpicuous, as ſhe wiſhed and hoped, in the younger part of her ſon's life ; yet there is great reaſon to believe, they were not entirely loſt. As they were probably the occaſion of many convictions, which in his younger years were over-borne ; ſo I doubt not, that when religious impreſſions took that ſtrong hold of his heart which they afterwards did, that ſtock of knowledge which had been ſo early laid up in his mind, was found of conſiderable ſervice. And I have heard him make the obſervation, as an encouragement to parents, and other pious friends, to do their duty, and to hope for thoſe good conſequences of it which may not immediately appear.

§. 11. Could his mother, or a very religious aunt, (of whole good inftructions and exhortations I have often heard him fpeak with pleafure,) have prevailed, he would not have thought of a military life, from which, it is no wonder, thefe ladies endeavoured to diffuade him, confidering the mournful experience they had of the dangers attending it, and the dear relatives they had loft already by it. But it fuited his tafte ; and the ardor of his fpirit, animated by the perfuafions of a friend who greatly urged it,* was not to be reftrained. Nor will the reader wonder, that thus excited and fupported, it eafily overbore their tender remonftrances, when he knows, that this lively youth fought three duels before he attained to the ftature of a man ; in one of which, when he was but eight years old, he received from a boy much older than himfelf, a wound in his right check, the fcar of which was always very apparent. The falfe fenfe of honour which inftigated him to it, might feem indeed fomething excufeable, in thofe unripened years, and confidering the profeffion of his father, brother, and uncle; but I have often heard him mention this rafhnefs with that regret, which the reflection would naturally give to fo wife and good a man in the maturity of life. And I have been informed, that after his remarkable converfion, he declined accepting a challenge, with this calm and truly great reply, which in a man of his experienced bravery was exceeding graceful ; " I fear finning, though you know I do not fear fighting."

§. 12. He ferved firft as a cadet which muft have been very early ; and then at 14 years old, he bore an enfign's commiffion in a Scotch regiment in the Dutch fervice ; in which he continued till the year 1702, when (if my information be right,) he received an enfign's commiffion from Queen Anne, which he bore in the battle of Ramellies, being then in the 19th year of his age. In this ever memorable action, he received a wound in his mouth by a mufket-ball, which hath often been reported to be the occafion of his converfion. That report was a miftaken one ; but as fome very remarkable circumftances attended this affair, which I have had the pleafure of hearing more than once from his own mouth, I hope my reader will excufe me, if I give him fo uncommon a ftory at large.

* I fuppofe this to have been Brigadier General Rue, who had from his childhood a peculiar affection for him.

§. 13. Our young officer was of a party in the forlorn hope, and was commanded on what seemed almost a desperate service, to dispossess the French of the church-yard at Ramellies, where a considerable number of them were posted to remarkable advantage. They succeeded much better than was expected; and it may well be supposed that Mr. Gardiner, who had before been in several encounters, and had the view of making his fortune to animate the natural intrepidity of his spirit, was glad of such an opportunity of signalizing himself, accordingly he had planted his colours on an advanced ground; and while he was calling to his men, (probably in that horrid language, which is so peculiar a disgrace to our soldiery, and so absurdly common in such articles of extreme danger,) he received a shot into his mouth; which, without beating out any of his teeth, or touching the fore-part of his tongue, went through his neck, and came out about an inch and an half on the left-side of the vertebræ. Not feeling at first the pain of the stroke, he wondered what was become of the ball, and in the wilderness of his surprize began to suspect he had swallowed it; but dropping soon after, he traced the passage of it by his finger, when he could discover it no other way: which I mention as one circumstance, among many which occur, to make it probable that the greater part of those who fall in battle by these instruments of death, feel very litttle anguish from the most mortal wounds.

§. 14. This accident happened about five or six in the evening, on the 23d day of May, in the year 1706; and the army pursuing its advantages against the French, without ever regarding the wounded (which was it seems the Duke of Marlborough's constant method) our young officer lay all night in the field; agitated as may well be supposed, with a great variety of thoughts. He assured me, that when he reflected upon the circumstances of his wound, that a ball should, as he then conceived it, go through his head without killing him, he thought God had preserved him by miracle; and therefore assuredly concluded, that he should live, abandoned and desperate as his state then seemed to be. Yet, (which to me appeared very astonishing) he had little thoughts of humbling himself before God, and returning to him after the wanderings of a life so licentiously begun.

But expecting to recover, his mind was taken up with contrivances to secure his gold, of which he had a pretty deal about him ; and he had recourse to a very odd expedient, which proved successful. Expecting to be stripped, he first took out a handful of that clotted gore, of which he was frequently obliged to clear his mouth, or he would have been choaked ; and putting it into his left-hand, he took out his money (which I think, was about nineteen pistoles) and shutting his hand, and besmearing the back part of it with blood, he kept it in this position till the blood dried in such a manner, that his hand could not easily fall open, though any sudden surprize should happen, in which he might lose the presence of mind which that concealment otherwise would have required.

§. 15. In the morning the French, who were masters of the spot, though their forces were defeated at some distance, came to plunder the slain ; and seeing him to appearance almost expiring, one of them was just applying a sword to his breast, to destroy the little remainder of life ; when in the critical moment, upon which all the extraordinary events of such a life as his afterwards proved were suspended, a cordelier, who attended the plunderers, interposed, taking him by his dress for a Frenchman ; and said, "Do not kill that poor child." Our young soldier heard all that passed, though he was not able to speak one word ; and opening his eyes, made a sign for something to drink They gave him a sup of some spirituous liquor, which happened to be at hand ; by which he said he found a more sensible refreshment, than he could remember from any thing he had tasted either before or since. Then signing to the friar to lean down his ear to his mouth, he employed the first efforts of his feeble breath in telling him (what, alas was a contrived falsehood) that he was nephew to the governor of Huy, a neutral town in the neighbourhood, and that, if he could take any method of conveying him thither, he did not doubt but his uncle would liberally reward him. He had indeed a friend at Huy, (who I think, was governor, and, if I mistake not, had been acquainted with the captain his father) from whom he expected a kind reception : but the relation was only pretended. On hearing this, they laid him on a sort of hand-barrow, and sent him by a file of musqueteers towards the

place; but the men loſt their way, and got into a wood towards the evening, in which they were obliged to continue
all night. The poor patient's wound being ſtill undreſſed,
it is not to be wondered that by this time it raged violently.

The anguiſh of it engaged him earneſtly to beg that they
would either kill him outright, or leave him there to die,
without the torture of any farther motion; and indeed they
were obliged to reſt for a conſiderable time, on account of
their own wearineſs. Thus he ſpent the ſecond night in
the open air, without any thing more than a common ban-
dage to ſtanch the blood. He hath often mentioned it as a
moſt aſtoniſhing providence, that he did not bleed to death;
which, under God, he aſcribed to the remarkable coldneſs
of theſe two nights.

§. 16. Judging it quite unſafe to attempt carrying him to
Huy, from whence they were now ſeveral miles diſtant, his
convoy took him early in the morning to a convent in the
neighbourhood; where he was hoſpitably received, and treated with great kindneſs and tenderneſs. But the cure of his
wound was committed to an ignorant barber ſurgeon, who
lived near the houſe; the beſt ſhift that could then be made,
at a time when it may eaſily be ſuppoſed perſons of ability
in their profeſſion had their hands full of employment. The
tent which this artiſt applied, was almoſt like a peg driven
into the wound; and gentlemen of ſkill and experience,
when they came to hear of the manner in which he was treated, wondered how he could poſſibly ſurvive ſuch management.
But by the bleſſing of God on theſe applications, rough as
they were, he recovered in a few months. The lady ab-
beſs, who called him her ſon, treated him with the
affection and care of a mother; and he always declared,
that every thing which he ſaw within theſe walls, was
conducted with the ſtricteſt decency and decorum. He
received a great many devout admonitions from the ladies
there; and they would fain have perſuaded him to acknowledge what they thought ſo miraculous a deliverance, by em-
bracing the catholic faith, as they were pleaſed to call it.
But they could not ſucceed: for though no religion lay near
his heart, yet he had too much of the ſpirit of a gentleman,
lightly to change that form of religion, which he wore (as
it were) looſe about him; as well as too much good ſenſe,
to ſwallow thoſe monſtrous abſurdities of popery, which im-

mediately prefented themfelves to him, unacquainted as he was with the niceties of the controverfy.

§ 17. When his liberty was regained by an exchange of prifoners, and his health thoroughly eftablifhed, he was far from rendering unto the Lord according to that wonderful difplay of divine mercy which he had experienced. I know very little of the particulars of thofe wild, thoughtlefs, and wretched years, which lay between the 19th and the 30th of his life; except it be, that he frequently experienced the divine goodnefs in renewed inftances, particularly in preferving him in feveral hot military actions in all which he never received fo much as a wound after this, forward as he was in tempting danger: and yet, that all thefe years were fpent in an entire alienation from God, and an eager purfuit of animal pleafure, as his fupreme good. The feries of criminal amours in which he was almoft inceffantly engaged during this time, muft probably have afforded fome remarkable adventures and occurrences; but the memory of them is perifhed. Nor do I think it unworthy notice here, that amidft all the intimacy of our friendfhip, and the many hours of chearful, as well as ferious converfe, which we fpent together, I never remember to have heard him fpeak of any of thefe intrigues, otherwife than in the general with deep and folemn abhorrence. This I the rather mention, as it feemed a moft genuine proof of his unfeigned repentance; which, I think, there is great reafon to fufpect, when people feem to take a pleafure in relating and defcribing fcenes of vicious indulgence, which yet they profefs to have difapproved and forfaken.

§. 18. Amidft all thefe pernicious wanderings from the paths of religion, virtue, and happinefs, he approved himfelf fo well in his military character, that he was made a lieutenant in that year, viz. 1706; And I am told, he was very quickly after promoted to a cornet's commiffion in lord Stair's regiment of the Scotch greys; and on the 31ft of January, in the year 1714-15, was made captain lieutenant in Colonel Ker's regiment of dragoons. He had the honour of being known to the Earl of Stair fome time before, and was made his aid de-camp; and when, upon his lordfhip's being appointed ambaffador from his late majefty to the court of France, he made fo fplendid an entrance into Paris, Captain Gardiner was his mafter of the horfe;

and I have been told, that a great deal of the care of that admirably well adjuſted ceremony fell upon him ; ſo that he gained great credit by the manner in which he conducted it. Under the benign influences of his lordſhip's favour, (which to the laſt day of his life he retained,) a captain's commiſſion was procured for him, (dated July 22, in the year 1715,) in the regiment of dragoons commanded by Colonel Stanhope, (now Earl of Harrington;) and, in the year 1717, he was advanced to the majority of that regiment ; in which office he continued till it was reduced, on November the 10th, 1718; when he was put out of commiſſion. But then his majeſty King George I. was ſo thoroughly apprized of his faithful and important ſervices, that he gave him his ſign-manual, intituling him to the firſt majority that ſhould become vacant, in any regiment of horſe or dragoons ; which happened, about five years after, to be in Croft's regiment of dragoons, in which he received a commiſſion, dated June the 1ſt, 1724; and on the 20th of July the ſame year, he was made major of an older regiment, commanded by the Earl of Stair.

§. 19. As I am now ſpeaking of ſo many of his military preferments, I will diſpatch the account of them by obſerving, that on the 24th of January, 1729-30, he was advanced to the rank of lieutenant-colonel in the ſame regiment, long under the command of Lord Cadogan ; with whoſe friendſhip this brave and vigilant officer was alſo honoured for many years. And he continued in this rank, and regiment, till the 19th of April, 1743, when he received a colonel's commiſſion over a regiment of dragoons, lately commanded by Brigadier Bland ; at the head of which he valiantly fell, in the defence of his ſovereign and his country, about two years and an half after he received it.

§. 20. We will now return to that period of his life which paſſed at Paris, the ſcene of ſuch remarkable and important events. He continued (if I remember right,) ſeveral years under the roof of the brave and generous Earl of Stair ; to whom he endeavoured to approve himſelf by every inſtance of diligent and faithful ſervice. And his lordſhip gave no inconſiderable proof of the dependance which he had upon him, when, in the beginning of the year 1715, he intruſted him with the important diſpatches, relating to a diſcovery, which by a ſeries of admirable policy he had made, of a defign which the French king was then forming, for invading Great-Britain in favour of the pretender ; in which the French apprehended they were fo fure of fuccefs, that it feemed a point of friendfhip in one of the chief counfellors of that court, to diffuade a dependant of his from accepting fome employment under his Britannic majefty, when propofed by his envoy there ; becaufe it was faid, that in lefs than fix weeks there would be a revolution, in favour of what they called the family of the Stuarts. The captain difpatched his journey with the utmoft fpeed ; a variety of circumftances happily concurred to accelerate it ; and they, who remember how foon the regiments which that emergency required were raifed and armed, will, I doubt not, efteem it a memorable inftance, both of the moft cordial zeal in the friends of the government, and of the gracious care of divine providence over the houfe of Hanover, and the Britifh liberties, fo infeparably connected with its intereft.

§. 21. While Captain Gardiner was at London, in one of the journies he made upon this occafion, he, with that franknefs which was natural to him, and which in thofe days was not always under the moft prudent reftraint, ventured to predict, from what he knew of the bad ftate of the French king's health that he would not live fix weeks. This was made known by fome fpies who were at St. James's, and came to be reported at the court of Verfailles ; for he received letters from fome friends at Paris, advifing him not to return thither, unlefs he could reconcile himfelf to a lodging in the baftile. But he was foon free from that apprehenfion ; for, if I miftake not, before half that time was accomplifhed, Louis XIV, died, Sept. 1, 1715, and it is generally thought, his death was haftened by a very accidental circumftance, which had fome reference to the captain's prophecy. For the laft time he ever dined in public, which was a very little while after the report of it had been made there, he happened to difcover our Britifh envoy among the fpectators. The penetration of this illuftrious perfon was too great, and his attachment to the intereft of his royal mafter too well known, not to render him very difagreeable to that crafty and tyrannical prince, whom God had fo long fuffered to be the difgrace of monarchy, and the fcourge of Europe. He at firft appeared very languid, as

B 2

indeed he was; but on caſting his eye upon the Earl of Stair, he affected to appear before him in a much better ſtate of health than he really was; and therefore, as if he had been awakened on a ſudden from ſome deep reverie, he immediately put himſelf into an erect poſture, called up a laboured vivacity into his countenance, and eat much more heartily than was by any means adviſeable, repeating it two or three times to a nobleman, (I think the Duke of Bourbon,) then in waiting, "Methinks I eat very well, for a "man who is to die ſo ſoon *." But this inroad upon that regularity of living, which he had for ſome time obſerved, agreed ſo ill with him, that he never recovered this meal, but died in leſs than a fortnight. This gave occaſion for ſome humorous people to ſay, that old Louis, after all, was killed by a Briton. But if this ſtory be true, (which I think there can be no room to doubt, as the colonel, from whom I have often heard it, though abſent, could ſcarce be miſinformed,) it might more properly be ſaid, that he fell by his own vanity; in which view I thought it ſo remarkable, as not to be unworthy a place in theſe memoirs.

§. 22. The captain quickly returned, and continued with ſmall interruptions at Paris, at leaſt till the year 1720, and how much longer I do not certainly know. The Earl's favor and generoſity made him eaſy in his affairs though he was (as has been obſerved above,) part of the time out of commiſſion, by breaking the regiment to which he belonged, of which before he was major. This was, in all probability, the gayeſt part of his life, and the moſt criminal. Whatever wiſe and good examples he might find in the family where he had the honour to reſide, it is certain that the French court, during the regency of the Duke of Orleans, was one of the moſt diſſolute under heaven. What, by a wretched abuſe of language, have been called intrigues of love and gallantry, were ſo entirely to the major's then degenerate taſte, that if not the whole buſineſs, at leaſt the whole happineſs of his life conſiſted in them; and he had now too much leiſure, for one who was ſo prone to abuſe it. His fine conſtitution, than which perhaps there was hardly ever a better, gave him great opportunities of indulging himſelf in theſe exceſſes; and his good ſpirits enabled him

---

* Il me ſemble, que je ne mange pas mal pour un homme qui devoit mourir ſi tôt.

to pursue his pleasures of every kind, in so alert and spright-
ly a manner, that multitudes envied him, and called him,
by a dreadful kind of compliment, " the Happy Rake."

§. 23. Yet still the checks of conscience, and some remaining principles of so good an education, would break in
upon his most licentious hours ; and I particularly remember he told me, that when some of his dissolute companions
were once congratulating him on his distinguished felicity,
a dog happening at that time to come into the room, he could
not forbear groaning inwardly, and saying to himself,
" Oh that I were that dog !" Such was then his happiness ;
and such perhaps is that of hundreds more, who bear themselves highest in the contempt of religion, and glory in that
infamous servitude which they affect to call liberty. But
these remonstrances of reason and conscience were in vain ;
and, in short, he carried things so far, in this wretched
part of his life, that I am well assured, some sober English
gentlemen, who made no great pretences to religion, how
agreeable soever he might have been to them on other accounts, rather declined than sought his company, as fearing
they might have been insnared and corrupted by it.

§. 24. Yet I cannot find, that in these most abandoned
days, he was fond of drinking. Indeed he never had any
natural relish for that kind of intemperance, from which he
used to think a manly pride might be sufficient to preserve
persons of sense and spirit ; as by it they give up every thing
that distinguishes them from the meanest of their species, or
indeed from animals the most below it. So that, if he
ever fell into any excesses of this kind, it was merely out
of complaisance to his company, and that he might not appear stiff and singular. His frank, obliging, and generous
temper, procured him many friends ; and these principles,
which rendered him amiable to others, not being under the
direction of true wisdom and piety, sometimes made him,
in the ways of living he pursued, more uneasy to himself,
than he might perhaps have been if he could entirely have
out-grown them ; especially as he was never a sceptic in his
principles, but still retained a secret apprehension, that natural and revealed religion, though he did not much care to
think of either, were founded in truth. And with this conviction, his notorious violations of the most essential precepts of both could not but occasion some secret misgivings

of heart. His continual neglect of the great Author of his being, of whoſe perfections he could not doubt, and to whom he knew himſelf to be under daily and perpetual obligations, gave him, in ſome moments of involuntary reflection, inexpreſſible remorſe; and this, at times, wrought upon him to ſuch a degree, that he reſolved he would attempt to pay him ſome acknowledgements. Accordingly for a few mornings he did it; repeating in retirement ſome paſſages out of the Pſalms, and perhaps other ſcriptures, which he ſtill retained in his memory; and owning, in a few ſtrong words, the many mercies and deliverances he had received, and the ill returns he had made for them.

§. 25. I find, among the other papers tranſmitted to me, the following verſes, which I have heard him repeat, as what had impreſſed him a good deal in his unconverted ſtate: and as I ſuppoſe they did ſomething towards ſetting him on this effort towards devotion, and might probably furniſh out a part of theſe oriſons, I hope I need make no apology to my reader for inſerting them, eſpecially as I do not recollect that I have ſeen them any where elſe,

Attend, my ſoul! The early birds inſpire
My grov'ling thoughts with pure celeſtial fire:
They from their temp'rate ſleep awake, and pay
Their thankful anthems for the new-born day.
See, how the tuneful lark is mounted high,
And, poet-like, ſalutes the eaſtern ſky!
He warbles through the fragrant air his lays,
And ſeems the beauties of the morn to praiſe.
But man, more void of gratitude, awakes,
And gives no thanks for the ſweet reſt he takes;
Looks on the glorious ſun's new-kindled flame,
Without one thought of Him from whom it came.
The wretch unhallow'd does the day begin;
Shakes off his ſleep, but ſhakes not off his ſin.

§. 26. But theſe ſtrains were too devout to continue long in a heart as yet quite unſanctified: For how readily ſoever he could repeat ſuch acknowledgments of the divine power, preſence, and goodneſs, and own his own follies and faults; he was ſtopt ſhort by the remonſtrances of his conſcience, as to the flagrant abſurdity, of confeſſing ſins he did not deſire to forsake, and of pretending to praise God for his mercies, when he did not endeavour to live to his service, and to behave in such a manner as gratitude, if sincere, would plainly dictate   A model of devotion, where such sentiments made no part, his good sense could not digest ; and the use of such language before an heart searching God, merely as an hypocritical form, while the sentiments of his soul were contrary to it, justly appeared to him such daring profaneness, that, irregular as the state of his mind was, the thought of it struck him with horror.   He therefore determined to make no more attempts of this sort ; and was perhaps one of the first, that deliberately laid aside prayer, from some sense of God's omniscience, and some natural principle of honour and conscience.

§. 27. These secret debates with himself, and ineffectual efforts, would sometimes return : but they were over-borne again and again, by the force of temptation ; and it is no wonder, that in consequence of them his heart grew yet harder.   Nor was it softened, or awakened, by some very memorable deliverances, which at this time he received.— He was in extreme danger by a fall from his horse, as he was riding post, (i think in the streets of Calais) when going down a hill, the horse threw him over his head, and pitched over him ; so that when he rose, the beast lay beyond him, and almost dead.   Yet, though he received not the least harm, it made no serious impression on his mind.— In his return from England in the packet-boat, (if I remember right, but a few weeks after the former accident,) a violent storm, that drove them up to Harwich, tossed them from thence for several hours in a dark night on the coast of Holland, and brought them into such extremity, that the captain of the vessel urged him to go to prayers immediately, if he ever intended to do it at all ; for he concluded, they would in a few minutes be at the bottom of the sea.   In this circumstance, he did pray, and that very fervently too : and it was very remarkable, that while he was crying to God for deliverance, the wind fell, and quickly after they arrived at Calais.   But the major was so little affected with what had befallen him, that when some of his gay friends, on hearing the story, rallied him upon the efficacy of his prayers, he excused himself from the scandal of being thought much in earnest, by saying, " that it was at midnight, an hour when

" his good mother and aunt were aſleep; or elſe he ſhould
" have left that part of the buſineſs to them." A ſpeech,
which I ſhould not have mentioned, but as it ſhews in ſo
lively a view the wretched ſituation of his mind at that
time, though his great deliverance from the power of darkneſs was then nearly approaching. He recounted theſe
things to me with the greateſt humility, as ſhewing how utterly unworthy he was of that miracle of divine grace, by
which he was quickly after brought to ſo true, and ſo pre-
valent, a ſenſe of religion.

§. 28. And now I am come to that aſtoniſhing part of his
ſtory, the account of his Converſion; which I cannot enter
upon without aſſuring my reader, that I have ſometimes been
tempted to ſuppreſs many circumſtances of it, not only, as
they may ſeem incredible to ſome, and enthuſiaſtical to others;
but as I am very ſenſible, they are liable to great abuſes;
which was the reaſon that he gave me, for concealing the
moſt extraordinary from many perſons, to whom he mentioned ſome of the reſt. And I believe it was this, together with the deſire of avoiding every thing that might look
like oſtentation on this head, that prevented his leaving a written account of it; though I have often entreated him to do
it: As I particularly remember I did, in the very laſt letter
I ever wrote him, and pleaded the poſſibility of his falling a-
midſt thoſe dangers, to which I knew his valour might in
ſuch circumſtances naturally expoſe him. I was not ſo happy as to receive any anſwer to this letter, which reached
him but a few days before his death: nor can I certainly ſay,
whether he had, or had not, complied with my requeſt;
as it is very poſſible, a paper of that kind, if it were written, might be loſt amidſt the ravages which the rebels made,
when they plundered Bankton.

§. 29. The ſtory however was ſo remaakable, that I had
little reaſon to apprehend I ſhould ever forget it; and yet, to
guard againſt all contingencies of that kind, I wrote it down
that very evening, as I had heard it from his own mouth: And
I have now before me the memoirs of that converſation, dated
Aug. 14, 1739, which conclude with theſe words; (which
I added, that if we ſhould both have died that night, the
world might not have loſt this edifying and affecting hiſtory, or have wanted any atteſtation of it I was capable of
giving;) " N, B. I have written down this account with

" all the exactness I am capable of, and could safely take an
" oath of it as to the truth of every circumstance, to the
" best of my remembrance, as the Colonel related it to me a
" few hours ago." I do not know, that I had reviewed
this paper since I wrote it, till I set myself thus publicly to
record this extraordinary fact; but I find it punctually to a-
gree with what I have often related from my memory, which
I charged carefully with so wonderful and important a fact.
It is with all solemnity that I now deliver it down to poste-
rity, as in the sight and presence of God. And I choose
deliberately to expose myself to those severe censures, which
the haughty, but empty, scorn of infidelity, or principles
nearly approaching it, and effectually doing its pernicious
work, may very probably dictate upon the occasion; rather
than to smother a relation, which may in the judgment of
my conscience, be like to conduce so much to the glory of
God, the honour of the gospel, and the good of mankind. One thing more I will only premise, that I hope,
none who have heard the Colonel himself speak something of
this wonderful scene, will be surprized if they find some new
circumstances here; because he assured me at the time he
first gave me the whole narration, (which was in the very
room in which I now write,) that he had never imparted it
so fully to any man living before. Yet. at the same time, he
gave me full liberty to communicate it to whomsoever I
should in my conscience judge it might be useful to do it, whether before, or after his death. Accordingly I did, while
he was alive, recount almost every circumstance I am now
going to write, to several pious friends; referring them at
the same time to the colonel himself, whenever they might
have an opportunity of seeing or writing to him, for a farther confirmation of what I told them, if they judged it requisite. They glorified God in him; and I humbly hope,
many of my readers will also do it. They will soon perceive the reason of so much caution in my introduction
to this story, for which therefore I shall make no further a-
pology."†

† It is no small satisfaction to me, since I wrote this, to have
received a letter from the Rev. Mr. Spears, Minister of the
gospel at Bruntisland, dated Jan. 14, 1746-7, in which he relates to me this whole story, as he had it from the Colonel's own
mouth, about four years after he gave me the narration. These

§. 30. This memorable event happened toward the middle of July, 1719, but I cannot be exact as to the day. The major had spent the evening (and if I miftake not, it was the Sabbath,) in fome gay company, and had an unhappy affignation with a married woman, of what rank or quality, I did not particularly enquire, whom he was to attend exactly at twelve. The company broke up about eleven; and not judging it convenient to anticipate the time appointed, he went into his chamber, to kill the tedious hour, perhaps with fome amufing book, or fome other way. But it very accidentally happened, that he took up a religious book, which his good mother or aunt had, without his knowledge, flipped into his portmanteau. It was called, if I remember the title exactly, The Chriftian Soldier, or Heaven taken by Storm; and was written by Mr. Thomas Watfon. Gueffing by the title of it, that he fhould find fome phrafes of his own profeffion fpiritualized, in a manner which he thought might afford him fome diverfion, he refolved to dip into it: but he took no ferious notice of any thing he read in it: And yet, while this book was in his hand, an impreffion was made upon his mind (perhaps God only knows how,) which drew after it a train of the moft important and happy confequences.

§ 31. There is indeed a poffibility, that while he was fitting in this attitude, and reading in this carelefs and profane manner, he might fuddenly fall afleep, and only dream of what he apprehended he faw. But nothing can be more certain, than that, when he gave me this relation, he judged himfelf to have been as broad awake during the whole time, as he ever was in any part of his life; and he mentioned it to me feveral times afterwards, as what undoubt-

is not a fingle circumftance, in which either of our narrations difagree; and every one of the particulars in mine, which feem moft aftonifhing, are attefted by this, and fometimes in ftronger words; one only excepted, on which I fhall add a fhort remark when I come to it. As this letter was written near lady Frances Gardiner, at her defire, and attended with a poftfcript from her own hand, this is in effect a fufficient atteftation, how agreeable it was to thofe accounts which fhe muft have often heard the Colonel give of this matter.

edly paſſed, not only in his imagination, but before his eyes. †

§. 32. He thought he ſaw an unuſual blaze of light fall on the book while he was reading, which he at firſt imagined might happen by ſome accident in the candle. But lifting up his eyes, he apprehended, to his extreme amazement, that there was before him, as it were ſuſpended in the air, a viſible repreſentation of the Lord Jeſus Chriſt upon the croſs, ſurrounded on all ſides with a glory; and was impreſſed, as if a voice, or ſomething equivalent to a voice, had come to him, to this effect; (for he was not confident as to the very words,) " Oh ſinner, did I ſuffer this for thee, " and are theſe the returns?" But whether this were an audible voice, or only a ſtrong impreſſion on his mind equally ſtriking. he did not ſeem very confident; though, to the beſt of my remembrance, he rather judged it to be the former. Struck with ſo amazing a phænomenon as this, there remained hardly any life in him, ſo that he ſunk down in the arm-chair in which he ſat, and continued, he knew not exactly how long, inſenſible; (which was one circumſtance, that made me ſeveral times take the liberty to ſuggeſt, that he might poſſibly be all this while aſleep:) but however that were, he quickly after opened his eyes, and ſaw nothing more than uſual.

§. 33. It may eaſily be ſuppoſed, he was in no condition to make any obſervation upon the time. in which he had remained in an inſenſible ſtate. Nor did he, throughout all the remainder of the night, once recollect that criminal and deteſtable aſſignation, which had before engroſſed all his

C

† Mr. Spears, in the letter mentioned above, where he introduces the Colonel telling his own ſtory, has theſe words : " All " of a ſudden there was preſented in a very lively manner to " my view or to my mind, a repreſentation of my glorious Re- " deemer, &c."——And this gentleman adds, in a parentheſis, " It was ſo lively and ſtriking, that he could not tell, whether " it was to his bodily eyes, or to thoſe of his mind." This makes me think, that what I had ſaid to him on the Phænomena of viſions, apparitions, &c. [as being, when moſt real, ſuper- natural impreſſions on the imagination, rather than attended with any external object,] had ſome influence upon him. Yet ſtill it is evident, he looked upon this as a viſion, whether it were before the eyes, or in the mind, and not as a dream.

thoughts. He roſe in a tumult of paſſions, not to be conceived; and walked to and fro in his chamber, till he was
ready to drop down, in unutterable aſtoniſhment and agony
of heart; appearing to himſelf the vileſt monſter in the
creation of God, who had all his life-time been crucifying
Chriſt afreſh by his ſins, and now ſaw, as he aſſuredly believed, by a miraculous viſion, the horror of what he had
done. With this was connected ſuch a view, both of the
majeſty and goodneſs of God, as cauſed him to loath and
abhor himſelf, and to repent as in duſt and aſhes. He immediately gave judgment againſt himſelf, that he was moſt
juſtly worthy of eternal damnation: He was aſtoniſhed,
that he had not been immediately ſtruck dead in the midſt
of his wickedneſs: And (which I think deſerves particular
remark,) though he aſſuredly believed that he ſhould ere
long be in hell, and ſettled it as a point with himſelf for ſeveral months, that the wiſdom and juſtice of God did almoſt
neceſſarily require, that ſuch an enormous ſinner ſhould be
made an example of everlaſting vengeance, and a ſpectacle
as ſuch both to angels and men, ſo that he hardly durſt pre-
ſume to pray for pardon; yet what he then ſuffered, was
not ſo much from the fear of hell, though he concluded it
would ſoon be his portion, as from a ſenſe of that horrible
ingratitude he had ſhewn to the God of his life, and to that
bleſſed Redeemer, who had been in ſo affecting a manner
ſet forth as crucified before him.

§. 34. To this he refers in a letter, dated from Douglas,
April 1, 1725, communicated to me by his lady*, but I
know not to whom it was addreſſed. His words are theſe:
" One thing relating to my converſion, and a remarkable
" inſtance of the goodneſs of God to me the chief of ſinners,

* N. B. Where I make any extracts as from Colonel Gardiner's letters, they are either from originals, which I have in
my own hands, or from copies, which were tranſmitted to me
from perſons of undoubted credit, chiefly by the right honorable
the lady Frances Gardiner, through the hand of the Rev. Mr.
Webſter, one of the miniſters of Edinburgh. This I the rather mention, becauſe ſome letters have been brought to me as Colonel
Gardiner's, concerning which, I have not only been very dubious, but morally certain, that they could not have been written
by him. I have alſo heard of many, who have been fond of aſſuring the world, that they were well acquainted with him, and
were near him when he fell; whoſe reports have been moſt in-

" I do not remember that I ever told to any other perfon.
" It was this ; that after the aftonifhing fight I had of my
" bleffed Lord, the terrible condition in which I was, pro-
" ceeded not fo much from the terrors of the law, as from a
" fenfe of having been fo ungrateful a monfter to him whom
" I thought I faw pierced for my tranfgreffions." I the
rather infert thefe words, as they evidently atteft the circumftance which may feem moft amazing in this affair, and
contain fo exprefs a declaration of his own apprehenfion
concerning it.

§. 35 In this view it may naturally be fuppofed, that
he paffed the remainder of the night waking ; and he could
get but little reft in feveral that followed. His mind was
continually taken up in reflecting on the divine purity and
goodnefs ; the grace which had been pro ofed to him in the
gofpel, and which he had rejected ; the fingular advantages
he had enjoyed and abufed ; and the many favours of providence which he had received, particularly in refcuing him
from fo many eminent dangers of death, which he now faw
muft have been attended with fuch dreadful and hopelefs de-
ftruction. The privileges of his education, which he had
fo much defpifed, now lay with an almoft infupportable
weight on his mind ; and the folly of that career of finful
pleafure, which he had fo many years been running with
defperate eagernefs and unworthy delight, now filled him
with indignation againft himfelf, and againft the great de-
ceiver, by whom (to ufe his own phrafe,) he had been " fo
wretchedly and fcandaloufly befooled." This he ufed often
to exprefs in the ftrongeft terms ; which I fhall not repeat
fo particularly, as i cannot recollect fome of them. But on
the whole, it is certain, that by what paffed before he left
his chamber the next day, the whole frame and difpofition
of his foul was new-modelled and changed ; fo that he became, and continued to the laft day of h's exemplary and
truly chriftian life, the very reverfe of what he had been
before. A variety of particulars, which I am afterwards
to mention, will illuftrate this in the moft convincing man-

confiftent with each other, as well as contrary to that teftimony
relating to the circumftances of his death, which, on the whole,
appeared to me beyond controverfy the moft natural and authentic; from whence therefore, I fhall take my account of that
affecting fcene.

ner. But I cannot proceed to them, without p
to adore ſo illuſtrious an inſtance of the power
of divine grace, and intreating my reader ſeri
upon it, that his own heart may be ſuitably a
ſurely if the truth of the fact be admitted,
views in which it can be placed, (that is, ſupp
impreſſion to have paſſed in a dream,) it muſt
have been little, if any thing, leſs than miracu
not in the courſe of nature be imagined, how
ſhould ariſe in a mind, full of the moſt impur
ſections, and (as he himſelf often pleaded.) r
from the thoughts of a crucified Saviour, than
ther object that can be conceived : Nor can v
poſe, it ſhould, without a mighty energy of the
be effectual to produce, not only ſome tranſient
ſion, but ſo entire and ſo permanent a change
and conduct.   ·

§. 36. On the whole therefore, I muſt beg
preſs my own ſentiments of the matter, by
this occaſion what I wrote ſeveral years ago,
ſermon on regeneration, in a paſſage dictated
circumſtantial knowledge which I had of this a
and methinks ſufficiently vindicated by it, if i
ly alone ; which yet, I muſt take the liberty
not : for I hope the world will be particula
that there is at leaſt a ſecond, that very near
it, whenever the eſtabliſhed church of Engl
one of its brighteſt living ornaments, and on
uſeful members, which that, or perhaps any
communion, can boaſt: In the mean time, in
plary life be long continued, and his zealous
dantly proſpered ! I beg my reader's pardon f
ſion. The paſſage I referred to above is remar
not equally, applicable to both the caſes, as
page 263, of the firſt edition, and page 166,
under that head, where I am ſhewing that (
accompliſhes the great work of which we ſpe
and immediate impreſſions on the mind. A
illuſtrations, there are the following words,
colonel's converſion will throw the juſteſt I
" I have known thoſe of diſtinguiſhed genius
" ners, and great experience in human affair

" having outgrown all the impreffions of a religious educa-
" tion ; after having been hardened, rather than fubdued,
" by the moft fingular mercies, even various, repeated,
" and aftonifhing deliverances, which have appeared to
" themfelves no lefs than miraculous ; after having lived for
" years without God in the world, notorioufly corrupt
" themfelves, and labouring to the utmoft to corrupt others ;
" have been ftopt on a fudden in the full career of their fin,
" and have felt fuch rays of the divine prefence, and of re-
" deeming love, darting in upon their minds, almoft like
" lightning from heaven, as have at once rouzed, overpow-
" ered, and transformed them : So that they have come out
" of their fecret chambers with an irreconcileable enmity to
" thofe vices, to which, when they entered them, they
" were the tameft and moft abandoned flaves ; and have ap-
" peared from that very hour the votaries, the patrons, the
" champions of religion ; and after a courfe of the moft re-
" folute attachment to it, in fpite of all the reafonings or
" the railleries, the importunities or the reproaches, of its
" enemies, they have continued to this day fome of its
" brighteft ornaments : A change, which I behold with e-
" qual wonder and delight, and which, if a nation fhould
" join in deriding it, I would adore as the finger of God."

§. 37. The mind of major Gardiner continued from this
remarkable time till towards the end of October (that is,
rather more than three months, but efpecially the two firft
of them,) in as extraordinary a fituation as one can well
imagine ; he knew nothing of the joys arifing from a fenfe
of pardon ; but on the contrary, for the greater part of that
time, and with very fhort intervals of hope toward the end
of it, took it for granted, that he muft, in all probability,
quickly perifh. Neverthelefs he had fuch a fenfe of the
evil of fin, of the goodnefs of the divine being, and of the
admirable tendency of the chriftian revelation, that he refolved to fpend the remainder of his life, while God continued him out of hell, in as rational and as ufeful a manner
as he could ; and to continue cafting himfelf at the feet of
divine mercy, every day, and often in a day, if peradven-
ture there might be hope of pardon, of which all that he
could fay was, that he did not abfolutely defpair. He had
at that time fuch a fenfe of the degeneracy of his own heart,

that he hardly durst form any determinate resolution against
sin, or pretend to engage himself by any vow in the presence of God; but he was continually crying to him, that
he would deliver him from the bondage of corruption. He
perceived in himself a most surprizing alteration with regard
to the dispositions of his heart; so that, though he felt little
of the delight of religious duties, he extremely desired opportunities of being engaged in them; and those licentious
pleasures, which had before been his heaven, were now
absolutely his aversion. And indeed, when I consider how
habitual those criminal indulgences were grown to him, and
that he was now in the prime of life, and all this while in
high health too, I cannot but be astonished to reflect upon
it, that he should be so wonderfully sanctified in body, as
well as in his soul and spirit, as that, for all the future
years of his life, he, from that hour, should find so constant
a disinclination to, and abhorance of, those criminal sensu-
alities, to which he fancied he was before so invincibly im-
pelled by his very constitution, that he was used strangely
to think and to say, that omnipotence itself could not reform
him, without destroying that body, and giving him another.*

---

* Mr. Spears expresses this wonderful circumstance in these
remarkable words: "I was (said the colonel to me,) effectually
"cured of all inclination to that sin I was so strongly addicted to,
"that I thought nothing but shooting me through the head could
"have cured me of it; and all desire and inclination to it was re-
"moved, as entirely as if it had been a sucking-child; nor did the
"temptation return to this day." Mr. Webster's words on the
same subject are these: "One thing I have heard the Colonel fre-
"quently say, that he was much addicted to impurity before his
"acquaintance with religion; but that so soon as he was enlight-
"ened from above, he felt the power of the Holy Ghost changing
"his nature so wonderfully, that his sanctification in this respect
"seemed more remarkable, than in any other." On which that
worthy person makes this very reasonable reflection. "So tho-
",rough a change of such a polluted nature, evidenced by the
"most unblemished walk and conversation for a long course of
"years, demonstrates indeed the power of the highest, and
"leaves no room to doubt of its reality." Mr. Spears says this
happened in three days time: but from what I can recollect,
all that the Colonel could mean by that expression, if he used it,
(as I conclude he did,) was, that he began to make the observation in the space of three days; whereas, during that time, his
thoughts were so taken up with the wonderful views present-
ed to his mind, that he did not immediately attend to it. If he

§. 38. Nor was he only delivered from that bondage of corruption, which had bee habitual to him for so many years, but he felt in his breast so contrary a difposition, that he was grieved to fee human nature, in thofe to whom he was moft entirely a ftranger, proftituted to fuch low and contemptible purfuits. He therefore exerted his natural courage in a very new kind of combat, and became an open advocate for religion, in all its principles, fo far as he was acquainted with them, and all its precepts, relating to fobriety, righteoufnefs, and godlinefs. Yet he was very defirous and cautious, that he might not run into an extreme, and made it one of his firft petitions to God, the very day after thefe amazing impreffions had been wrought in his mind, that he might not be fuffered to behave with fuch an affected ftrictnefs and precifenefs, as would lead others about him into miftaken notions of religion, and expofe it to reproach or fufpicion, as if it were an unlovely or uncomfortable thing. For this reafon he endeavoured to appear as chearful in converfation, as he confcientioufly could; though, in fpite of all his precautions, fome traces of that deep inward fenfe which he had of his guilt and mifery, would at times appear. He made no fecret of it however, that his views were entirely changed, though he concealed the particular circumftances attending that change. He told his moft intimate companions freely, that he had reflected on the courfe of life in which he had fo long joined them, and found it to be folly and madnefs, unworthy a rational creature, and much more unworthy perfons calling themfelves chriftians. And he fet up his ftandard, upon all occafions, againft principles of infidelity, and practices of vice, as determinately, and as boldly, as ever he difplayed or planted his colours, when he bore them with fo much honour in the field.

§. 39. I cannot forbear mentioning one ftruggle of this kind, which he defcribed to me, with a large detail of circumftances, the firft day of our acquaintance. There was at that time in Paris a certain lady, (whofe name, then

had within the firft three days any temptation to feek fome eafe from the anguifh of his mind, in returning to former fenfualities, it is a circumftance he did not mention to me; and by what I can recollect of the ftrain of his difcourfe, he intimated, if he did not exprefs the contrary.

well known in the grand and the gay world, I muſt beg
leave to conceal,) who had imbibed the principles of deiſm,
and valued herſelf much upon being an avowed advocate for
them.   The major, with his uſual frankneſs, (though I
doubt not with that politeneſs of manners, which was ſo
habitual to him, and which he retained throughout his whole
life,) anſwered her, like a man who perfectly ſaw through
the fallacy of her arguments, and was grieved to the heart
for her deluſion.   On this ſhe briſkly challenged him to debate the matter at large, and to fix upon a day for that purpoſe, when he ſhould dine with her, attended with any
clergyman he might chuſe, whether of the proteſtant, or
catholic communion.   A ſenſe of duty would not allow him
to decline this challenge ; and yet he had no ſooner accepted
it, but he was thrown into great perplexity and diſtreſs, left
being (as I remember he expreſſed it, when he told me the
ſtory,) only a chriſtian of ſix weeks old, he ſhould prejudice
ſo good a cauſe, by his unſkilful manner of defending it.
However, he ſought his refuge in earneſt and repeated prayers to God, that he who can ordain ſtrength, and perfect
praiſe, out of the mouth of babes and ſucklings, would gra-
ciouſly enable him, on this occaſion, to vindicate his truths
in a manner which might carry conviction along with it.
He then endeavoured to marſhal the arguments in his own
mind, as well as he could ; and apprehending that he
could not ſpeak with ſo much freedom before a number of
perſons, eſpecially before ſuch, whoſe province he might in
that caſe ſeem to invade, if he had not devolved the princi-
pal part of the diſcourſe upon them, he eaſily admitted the
apology of a clergyman or two, to whom he mentioned the
affair. and waited on the lady alone upon the day appointed.
But his heart was ſo ſet upon the buſineſs, that he came
earlier than he was expected, and time enough to have two
hours diſcourſe before dinner ; nor did he at all decline having two young perſons, nearly related to the lady, preſent
during the conference.

§. 40. The major opened it, with a view of ſuch arguments for the chriſtian religion as he had digeſted in his
own mind, to prove that the apoſtles were not miſtaken
themſelves, and that they could not have intended to impoſe
upon us, in the accounts they give of the grand facts they
atteſt ; with the truth of which facts, that of the chriſtian

religion is moſt apparently connected. And it was a great
encouragement to him, to find, that unaccuſtomed as he
was to diſcourſes of this nature, he had an unuſual command,
both of thought, and expreſſion; ſo that he recollected, and
uttered every thing, as he could have wiſhed. The lady
heard with attention; and though he pauſed between every
branch of the argument, ſhe did not interrupt the courſe of
it, till he told her, he had finiſhed his deſign, and waited
for her reply. She then produced ſome of her objections,
which he took up and canvaſſed in ſuch a manner, that at
length ſhe burſt out into tears, allowed the force of his arguments and replies, and appeared, for ſome time after, ſo
deeply impreſſed with the converſation, that it was obſerved
by ſeveral of her friends: and there is reaſon to believe, that
the impreſſion continued, at leaſt ſo far as to prevent her
from ever appearing under the character of an unbeliever or
a ſceptic.

§. 41. This is only one ſpecimen among many, of the
battles he was almoſt daily called out to fight, in the cauſe
of religion and virtue; with relation to which I find him
expreſſing himſelf thus, in a letter to Mrs. Gardiner his
good mother, dated from Paris, the 25th of January following, that is, 1719-20. in anſwer to one, in which ſhe had
warned him to expect ſuch trials. "I have (ſays he,) al-
"ready met with them, and am obliged to fight, and to diſ-
"pute every inch of ground: But all thanks and praiſe to the
"great Captain of my ſalvation, he fights for me; and then
"it is no wonder, that I come off more than conqueror;"
by which laſt expreſſion I ſuppoſe he meant to inſinuate,
that he was ſtrengthened and eſtabliſhed, rather than over-
borne by this oppoſition. Yet it was not immediately, that
he gained ſuch fortitude. He has often told me, how much
he felt in thoſe days, of the emphaſis of thoſe well-choſen
words of the apoſtle, in which he ranks the trial of cruel
mockings, with ſcourgings, and bonds, and impriſonments.
The continual railleries with which he was received, in almoſt all companies where he had been moſt familiar before, did
often diſtreſs him beyond meaſure; ſo that he has ſeveral
times declared, he would much rather have marched up to
a battery of the enemy's cannon, than have been obliged,
ſ continually as he was, to face ſuch artillery as this. But,
like a brave ſoldier in the firſt action wherein he is enga-

ged, he continued resolute, though shuddering at the terror of the assault; and quickly overcame those impressions, which it is not perhaps in nature wholly to avoid: And therefore I find him in the letter referred to above, which was written about half a year after his conversion, " quite ashamed to " think of the uneasiness which these things once gave him." In a word, he went on, as every resolute christian by divine grace may do, till he turned ridicule and opposition into respect and veneration.

§. 42. But this sensible triumph over these difficulties was not, till his christian experience had been abundantly advanced, by the blessing of God on the sermons he heard, (particularly in the Swiss chapel,) and on the many hours which he spent in devout retirement, pouring out his whole soul before God in prayer. He began, within about two months after his first memorable change, to perceive some secret dawnings of more chearful hope, that vile as he saw himself to be, (and I believe no words can express, how vile that was,) he might nevertheless obtain mercy through a Redeemer. And at length, (if I remember right, about the end of October, 1719,) he found all the burthen of his mind taken off at once, by the powerful impression of that memorable scripture upon his mind; Rom iii 25, 26. " Whom God hath " set forth for a propitiation, through faith in his blood, to " declare his righteousness in the remission of sins,—that he " might be just, and the justifier of him that believeth in je- " sus." He had used to imagine, that the justice of God required the damnation of so enormous a sinner, as he saw himself to be. But now he was made deeply sensible, that the divine justice might be, not only vindicated, but glorified, in saving him by the blood of Jesus, even that blood which " cleanseth us from all sin." Then did he see, and feel, the riches of redeeming love and grace, in such a manner, as not only engaged him, with the utmost pleasure and confidence to venture his soul upon it; but even swallowed up, (as it were) his whole heart in the returns of love, which from that blessed time became the genuine and delightful principle of his obedience, and animated him with an enlarged heart, to run the way of God's commandments. Thus God was pleased, (as he himself used to speak,) in an hour to turn his captivity. All the terrors of his former state were changed into unutterable joy, which kept him almost continually waking for three nights together, and yet refreshed him as the nobleft of cordials. His expreffions, though naturally very ftrong, always feemed to be fwallowed up, when he would defcribe the feries of thought through which he now paffed, under the rapturous experience of that joy unfpeakable, and full of glory, which then feemed to overflow his very foul ; as indeed there was nothing he feemed to fpeak of with greater relifh, And though the firft extafies of it afterwards fubfided into a more calm and compofed delight ; yet were the impreffions fo deep, and fo permanent, that he affured me, on the word of a chriftian and a friend, wonderful as it might feem, that for about feven years after this he enjoyed almoft an heaven upon earth. His foul was fo continually filled with a fenfe of the love of God in Chrift, that it knew little interruption, but when neceffary converfe, and the duties of his ftation, called off his thoughts for a little time : And when they did fo, as foon as he was alone, the torrent returned into its natural channel again ; fo that from the minute of his awakening in the morning, his heart was rifing to God, and triumphing in him ; and thefe thoughts attended him through all the fcenes of life, till he lay down on his bed again, and a fhort parenthefis of fleep (for it was but a very fhort one that he allowed himfelf,) invigorated his animal powers, for renewing them with greater intenfenefs and fenfibility.

§. 43. I fhall have an opportunity of illuftrating this in the moft convincing manner below, by extracts from feveral letters which he wrote to intimate friends during this happy period of time ; letters, which breathe a fpirit of fuch fublime and fervent piety, as I have feldom met with any where elfe. In thefe circumftances, it is no wonder, that he was greatly delighted with Doctor Watts's imitation of the 126th Pfalm ; fince it may be queftioned, whether there ever was a perfon, to whom the following ftanzas of it were more fuitable,

I.

When God reveal'd his gracious name,
And chang'd my mournful ftate,
My rapture feem'd a pleafing dream ;
The grace appear'd fo great.

II.

The world beheld the glorious change,
  And did thine hand confeſs ,
My to gue broke out in unknown ſtrains,
  And ſang ſurpriſing grace,

IiI.

" Great is the work, my neighbours cry'd,
  " And own'd the power divine :
" Great is the work," my heart reply'd,
  " And be the glory thine."

IV.

The Lord can change the darkeſt ſkies,
  Can g ve us day for night,
Make floods of ſacred ſorrow riſe
  To rivers of delight.

V.

Let thoſe that ſow in ſadneſs, wait,
  Till the fair harveſt come :
They ſhall confeſs their ſheaves are great,
  And ſhout the bleſſings home.

§. 44. I have been ſo happy as to get the ſight of five original letters, which he wrote to his mother about this time;
which do, in a very lively manner, illuſtrate the ſurpriſing change made in the whole current of his thoughts, and
temper of his mind. Many of them were written in the moſt
haſty manner, juſt as the courier who brought them was,
perhaps unexpectedly, ſetting out : and they relate chiefly
to affairs. in which the public is not at all concerned : Yet
there is not one of them, in which he has not inſerted ſome
warm and genuine ſentiment of religion. And indeed it is
very remarkable, that though he was pleaſed to honor me
with a great many letters, and I have ſeen ſeveral more
which he wrote to others, ſome of them on journeys, where
he could have but a few minutes at command ; yet I cannot
recollect, that I ever ſaw any one, in which there was not
ſome trace of piety. And the Rev. Mr. Webſter, who was
employed to review great numbers of them, that he might
ſelect ſuch extracts as he ſhould think proper to communicate to me, has made the ſame obſervation.*

* His words are theſe : " I have read over a vaſt number of
" the Colonel's letters, and have not found any one of them,
" however ſhort, and writ in the moſt paſſing manner, even

§. 45. The major, with great juſtice, tells the good lady his mother, "that when ſhe ſaw him again, ſhe would find "the perſon indeed the ſame, but every thing elſe entire- "ly changed." And ſhe might eaſily have perceived it of herſelf, by the whole tenor of theſe letters, which every, where breathe the unaffected ſpirit of a true chriſtian. They are taken up, ſometimes with giving advice and directions concerning ſome pious and charitable contributions ; (one of which I remember amounted to ten guineas, though, as he was then out of commiſſion, and had not formerly been very frugal, it cannot be ſuppoſed he had much to ſpare ;) ſometimes in ſpeaking of the pleaſure, with which he attend- ed ſermons, and expected ſacramental opportunities ; and at other times, in exhorting her, eſtabliſhed as ſhe was in re- ligion, to labour after a yet more examplary character and conduct, or in recommending her to the divine preſence and bleſſing, as well as himſelf to her prayers. What ſa- tisfaction ſuch letters as theſe muſt give to a lady of her diſtinguiſhed piety, who had ſo long wept over this dear and amiable ſon, as quite loſt to God, and on the verge of final deſtruction, it is not for me to deſcribe, or indeed to con- ceive. But haſtily as theſe letters were written, only for private view, I will give a few ſpecimens from them in his own words ; which will ſerve to illuſtrate, as well as con- firm what I have hinted above.

§. 46. " I muſt take the liberty," ſays he, in a letter dated on the firſt day of the new year, or according to the Old Style, December 21, 1719, " to intreat you that you " would receive no company on the Lord's day. I know, " you have a great many good acquaintance, with whoſe " diſcourſes one might be very well edified : But as you can- " not keep out, and let in, whom you pleaſe, the beſt way, " in my humble opinion, will be to ſee none " In another of Jan. 25. " I am happier than any one can imagine, " except I could put him exactly in the ſame ſituation with .

D

" when poſting, but what is expreſſive of the moſt paſſionate " breathings towards his God and Saviour. If the letter con- " ſiſts but of two ſentences, religion is not forgotten ; which " doubtleſs deſerves to be carefully remarked, as the moſt un- " conteſted evidence of a pious mind, ever under the warmeſt " impreſſiens of divine things."

" myſelf; which is what the world cannot give, and no
" man ever attained it, unleſs it were from above." In
another, dated March 30, which was juſt before a ſacrament day, " To-morrow, if it pleaſe God, I ſhall be hap-
" py; my ſoul being to be fed with the bread of life, which
" came down from heaven. I ſhall be mindful of you all
" there." In another of Jan. 29, he thus expreſſes that
indifference for worldly poſſeſſions, which he ſo remarkably
carried through all the remainder of his life ; " I know, the
" rich are only ſtewards for the poor, and muſt give an ac-
" count of every penny ; therefore the leſs I have, the
" more eaſy will it be to render a faithful account of it."
And to add no more from theſe letters at preſent, in the concluſion of one of them he has theſe comprehenſive and ſolemn words : " Now that He, who is the eaſe of the afflicted,
" the ſupport of the weak, the wealth of the poor, the teach-
" er of the ignorant, the anchor of the fearful, and the in-
" finite reward of all faithful ſouls, may pour out upon you
" all his richeſt bleſſings, ſhall always be the prayer of him
" who is entirely your's, &c."

§. 47. To this account of his correſpondence with his excellent mother, I ſhould be glad to add a large view of another, to which ſhe introduced him, with that reverend and
valuable perſon, under whoſe paſtoral care ſhe was placed,
I mean, the juſtly celebrated Doctor Edmund Calamy, to
whom ſhe could not but early communicate the joyful news
of her ſon's converſion. I am not ſo happy as to be poſſeſſed
of the letters, which paſſed between them, which I have
reaſon to believe would make a curious and valuable collec-
tion : But I have had the pleaſure of receiving from my
worthy and amiable friend, the Rev. Mr. Edmund Calamy,
one of the letters which the Doctor his father wrote to the
major on this wonderful occaſion. I perceive by the contents of it, that it was the firſt ; and indeed it is dated as
early as the third of Auguſt, 1719, which muſt be but a few
days after his own account, dated Aug. 4. N. S. could reach
England. There is ſo much true religion and good ſenſe
in this paper, and the counſel it ſuggeſts may be ſo ſeaſona-
ble to other perſons in circumſtances which bear any reſem-
blance to his, that I make no apology to my reader for inſerting a large extract from it.

§. 48. " Dear Sir,—I conceive it will not much furprize
" you to underſtand, that your good mother communicated
" to me your letter to her, dated Aug, 4. N. S, which
" brought her the news you conceive would be ſo acceptable
" to her. I, who have often been a witneſs to her con-
" cern for you on a ſpiritual account, can atteſt with what
" joy this news was received by her, and imparted to me
" as a ſpecial friend, who ſhe knew would bear a part with
" her on ſuch an occaſion. And indeed, if (as our Saviour
" intimates, Luke xv 7, 10.) there is in ſuch caſes joy in
" heaven, and among the angels of God, it may well be
" ſuppoſed, that of a pious mother, who has ſpent ſo many
" prayers and tears upon you and has as it were travailed
" in birth with you again, till Chriſt was formed in you,
" could not be ſmall. You may believe me if I add, that I
" alſo, as a common friend of her's and your's, and which
" is much more of the Prince of Light, whom you now de-
" clare you heartily fall in with, in oppoſition to that of the
" dark kingdom, could not but be tenderly affected with an
" account of it under your own hand. My joy on this ac-
" count was the greater, conſidering the importance of your
" capacity, intereſts, and proſpects; which, in ſuch an
" age as this, may promiſe moſt happy conſequences, on
" your heartily appearing on God's ſide, and embarking in
" the intereſt of our dear Redeemer. If I have hitherto at
" all remembered you at the throne of grace, at your good
" mother's deſire, (which you are pleaſed to take notice of
" with ſo much reſpect,) I can aſſure you i ſhall hence-for-
" ward be led to do it, with more concern and particulari-
" ty, both by duty and inclination And if I were capa-
" ble of giving you any little aſſiſtance in the noble deſign
" you are engaging in, by correſponding with you by letter,
" while you are at ſuch a diſtance, I ſhould do it moſt chear-
" fully. And perhaps, ſuch a motion may not be altoge-
" ther unacceptable: For I am inclinable to believe, that
" when ſome, whom you are obliged to converſe with, ob-
" ſerve your behaviour ſo different from what it formerly
" was, and banter you upon it as mad and fanciful, it may
" be ſome little relief to correſpond with one, who will
" take a pleaſure in heartening and encouraging you. And
" when a great many things frequently offer, in which con-
" ſcience may be concerned, where duty may not always

" be plain, nor ſuitable perſons to adviſe with at hand, it
" may be ſome ſatisfaction to you to correſpond with one,
" with whom you may uſe a friendly freedom in all ſuch
" matters, and on whoſe fidelity you may depend. You
" may therefore command me in any of theſe reſpects, and
" I ſhall take a pleaſure in ſerving you.   One piece of ad-
" vice I ſhall venture to give you, though your own good
" ſenſe will make my enlarging upon it leſs needful ; i mean
" that you would, from your firſt ſetting out carefully dif-
" tinguiſh between the eſſentials of real religion, and thoſe
" things which are commonly reckoned by its profeſſors to
" belong to it.   The want of this diſtinction has had very
" unhappy conſequences from one age to another, and per-
" haps in none more than the preſent.   But your daily con-
" verſe with your bible, which you mention, may herein
" give you great aſſiſtance,   I move alſo, that ſince infidel-
" ity ſo much.abounds, you would not only, by cloſe and
" ſerious conſideration, endeavour to ſettle yourſelf well
" in the fundamental principles of religion, but alſo that,
" as opportunity offers, you would converſe with thoſe books
" which treat moſt judiciouſly on the divine original of chriſ-
" tianity, ſuch as Grotius, Abadie, Baxter, Bates, Du
" Pleſſis, &c. which may eſtabliſh you againſt the cavils
" that occur in almoſt all converſations. and furniſh you with
" arguments which, when properly offered, may be of uſe
" to make ſome impreſſions on others.   But being too much
" ſtraitened to enlarge at preſent, I can only add, that if
" your hearty falling in with ſerious religion ſhould prove
" any hindrance to your advancement in the world, (which
" I pray God it may not, unleſs ſuch advancement would-
" be a real ſnare to you,) I hope you will truſt our Saviour's
" word, that it ſhall be no diſadvantage to you in the final
" iſſue : He has given you his word for it, Matt, xix. 29.
" upon which you may ſafely depend ; and I am ſa.isfied,
" none that ever did ſo at laſt repented of it.   May you go
" on and proſper, and the God of all grace and peace be
" with you !"

§. 49. I think it very evident from the contents of this
letter, that the major had not imparted to his mother the
moſt ſingular circumſtances attending his converſion : And
indeed, there was ſomething ſo peculiar in them, that I do
not wonder, he was always cautious in ſpeaking of them,

and efpecially, that he was at firft much on the referve. We may alfo naturally reflect, that there feems to have been fomething very providential in this letter, confidering the debate in which our illuftrious convert was fo foon engaged. For it was written but about three weeks. before his conference with the lady above mentioned in the defence of chriftianity ; or at leaft, before the appointment of it. And as fome of the books recommended by Dr. Calamy, particularly Abadie and Du Pleffis were undoubtedly within his reach, (if our Englifh advocates were not,) this might, by the divine bleffing contribute confiderably towards arming him for that combat, in which he came off with fuch happy fucceſs. And as in this inftance, fo in many others, they who will obferve the coincidence and concurrence of things, may be engaged to adore the wife conduct of providence in events, which, when taken fingly and by themfelves, have nothing very remarkable in them.

§ 50. I think it was about this time, that this refolute and examplary chriftian entered upon that methodical manner of living, which he purfued through fo many fucceeding years of life, and I believe, generally, fo far as the broken ftate of his health would allow it in his latter days, to the very end of it. He ufed conftantly to rife at four in the morning. and to fpend his time till fix in the fecret exercifes of devotion, reading, meditation, and prayer ; in which laft he contracted fuch a fervency of fpirit, as I believe few men living ever obtained. This certainly tended very much to ftrengthen that firm faith in God, and reverend animating fenfe of his prefence, for which he was fo eminently remarkable, and which carried him through the trials and fervices of life, with fuch fteadinefs, and with fuch activity ; for he indeed endured, and acted, as always feeing him who is invifible. If at any time he was obliged to go out before fix in the morning, he rofe proportionably fooner ; fo that when a journey, or a march, has required him to be on horfe back by four, he would be at his devotions at fartheft by two. He likewife fecured time for retirement in an evening ; and that he might have it the more at command, and be the more fit to ufe it properly. as well as the better able to rife early the next morning, he generally went to bed about ten : And, during the time I was

acquainted with him, he ſeldom eat any ſupper, but a mouth-
ful of bread with one glaſs of wine. In conſequence of this,
as well as of his admirably good conſtitution, and the long
habit he had formed, he required leſs ſleep than moſt perſons I have known : And I doubt not, but his uncommon
progreſs in piety was in a great meaſure owing to theſe re-
ſolute habits of ſelf-denial.

§. 51. A life any thing like this, could not, to be ſure,
be entered upon, in the midſt of ſuch company as he had
been accuſtomed to keep, without great oppoſition : Eſpecially, as he did not entirely withdraw himſelf from all the
circle of chearful converſation ; but on the contrary, gave ſeveral hours every day to it, left religion ſhould be reproach-
ed, as having made him moroſe. He however early began
a practice, which to the laſt day of his life he retained, of
reproving vice and profaneneſs ; and was never afraid to
debate the matter with any, under the conſciouſneſs of ſuch
ſuperiority in the goodneſs of his cauſe.

§. 52. A remarkable inſtance of this happened, if I miſ-
take not, about the middle of the year 1720, though I cannot be very exact as to the date of the ſtory. It was however on his firſt return, to make any conſiderable abode in
England, after this remarkable change. He had heard, on
the other ſide of the water, that it was currently reported
among his companions at home, that he was ſtark mad :
A report, at which no reader, who knows the wiſdom of
the world in theſe matters, will be much ſurprized, any
more than himſelf. He concluded therefore, that he ſhould
have many battles to fight, and was willing to diſpatch the
buſineſs as faſt as he could. And therefore, being to ſpend
a few days at the country houſe of a perſon of diſtinguiſhed
rank, with whom he had been very intimate, (whoſe name
I do not remember that he told me, nor did I think it proper to enquire after it,) he begged the favour of him that
he would contrive matters ſo, that a day or two after he
came down, ſeveral of their former gay companions might
meet at his lordſhip's table ; that he might have an appor-
tunity of making his apology to them, and acquainting them
with the nature and reaſons of his change. It was accordingly agreed to ; and a pretty large company met on the day
appointed, with previous notice that major Gardiner would
be there. A good deal of raillery paſſed at dinner, to which

very little anſwer. But when the cloth waſ
ıd the ſervants retired, he begged their pa-
v minutes, and then plainly and ſeriouſly
ıt notions he entertained of virtue and religi-
ıt conſiderations he had abſolutely determin-
grace of God he would make it the care and
whatever he might loſe by it, and whatever
tempt he might incur. He well knew how
in ſuch company, to relate the extraordinary
·h he was awakened; which they would pre-
·rpreted as a demonſtration of lunacy, againſt
ınd ſolidity of his diſcourſe : But he content-
ſuch a rational defence of a righteous, ſober,
as he knew none of ʼthem could with any
n conteſt. He then challenged them to pro-
·hey could urge, to prove that a life of irre-
ıchery was preferable to the fear, love, and
·ternal God, and a conduct agreeable to the
goſpel. And he failed not to bear his teſti-
own experience, (to one part of which many
·n witneſſes,) that after having run the wid-
ſual pleaſure, with all the advantages the beſt
ſpirits could give him, he had never taſted
ıeſerved to be called happineſs, till he had
ıis refuge and his delight. He teſtified calm-
the habitual ſerenity and peace that he now
breaſt, (for the moſt elevated delights he
t to plead, leaſt they ſhould be eſteemed en-
the compoſure and pleaſure with which he
to objects, which the gayeſt ſinner muſt ac-
e equally unavoidable and dreadful.
ɔw not what might be attempted by ſome of
ı anſwer to this; but I well remember he
after of the table, a perſon of a very frank
ıſition, cut ſhort the debate, and ſaid, "Come,
other cauſe : We thought this man mad, and
·arneſt proving that we are ſo." On the
ll judged circumſtance ſaved him a great deal
·. When his former acquaintance obſerved,
l converſable and innocently chearful, and
ımoveable in his, reſolutions, they deſiſted
ımportunity. And he has aſſured me that

inftead of lofing any one valuable friend by this change in his character, he found himfelf much more efteemed and re· garded, by many who could not perfuade themfelves to imi· tate his example.

§. 54. I have not any memoirs of Colonel Gardiner's life, or of any other remarkable event befalling him in it, from the time of his return to England, till his marriage in the year 1726; except the extracts which have been fent me from fome letters, which he wrote to his religious friends during this interval, and which I cannot pals by without a more particular notice. It may be recollected, that in con fequence of the reduction of that regiment of which he wa major he was out of commiffion from Nov. the 10th, 1718 till June the 1ft, 1724: And after he returned from Paris I find all his letters during this period dated from London, where he continued, in communion with the chriftian foci ety under the paftoral care of Doctor Calamy. As his goo mother alfo belonged to the fame, it is eafy to imagine, i mult be an unfpeakable pleafure to her, to have fuch frequen opportunities of converfi·g with fuch a fon, of obferving i his daily conduct and difcourfes the bleffed effects of tha change which divine grace had made in his heart, and o fitting down with him monthly at that facred feaft, wher chriftians fo frequently enjoy the divineft entertainment which they expect on this fide heaven. I the rather men tion this ordinance, becaufe as this excellent lady had a ve ry high efteem for it, fo fhe had an opportunity of attendin it, but the very Lords' day immediately preceding he death, which happened on Thurfday, Oct. 7, 1725, afte her fon had been removed from her almoft one year, H had maintained her handfomely out of that very moderate in come, on which he fubfifted fince his regiment had been dif banded; and when fhe expreffed her gratitude to him for it, h affured her, (I think, in one of the laft letters fhe ever re ceived from him,) "that he efteemed it a great honour " that God put it into his power, to make what he cal· " led, a very fmall acknowledgement of all her care fo " him, and efpecially of the many prayers fhe had offere " on his account, which had already been remarkably an " fwered, and the benefit of which he hoped ever to enjoy."

§. 55. I apprehend, that the Earl of Stair's regiment to the majority of which he was promoted on the 20th o

July, 1724, was then quartered in Scotland; for all the
letters in my hand from that time to the 6th of February,
1726, are dated from thence, and particularly from Douglas, Stranrawen, Hamilton, and Air: But I have the
pleasure to find, from comparing these with others of an
earlier date from London and the neighbouring parts that
neither the detriment which he must suffer by being so long
out of commission, nor the hurry of affairs while charged
with it, could prevent or interrupt that intercourse with
heaven, which was his daily feast, and his daily strength,

§. 56. These were most eminently the happy years of his
life : for he had learned to estimate his happiness, not by the
increase of honour, or the possession of wealth, or by what
was much dearer to his generous heart than either, the converse of the dearest and worthiest human friends; but by
nearness to God, and by opportunities of humble converse
with him in the lively exercise of contemplation, praise, and
prayer. Now there was no period of his life. in which he
was more eminently favoured with these; nor do . find any
of his letters so overflowing with transports of holy joy, as
these which were dated during this time. There are indeed
in some of them, such very sublime passages. that I have
been dubious, whether I should communicate then to the
public, or not; left I should administer matter of profane ridicule to some, who look upon all the elevations of devotion
as a contemptible enthusiasm. And it has also given me
some apprehensions, left it should discourage some pious Christians, who after having spent several years in the service of
God and in humble obedience to the precepts of his gospel,
may not have attained to any such heights as these. But on
the whole, I cannot satisfy myself to suppress them ; not
only as I number some of them considered in a devotional
view, among the most extraordinary pieces of the kind I
have ever met with ; but as some of the most excellent and
judicious persons I any where know, to whom I have read
them, have assured me, that they felt their hearts in an un-
usual manner impressed quickened, and edified by them,

§ 57. I will therefore draw back the veil and shew my
much honoured friend in his most secret recesses; that the
world may see, what those springs were, from whence issued
that clear, permanent, and living stream of wisdom, piety,
and virtue, which so apparently ran through all that part of

his life which was open to public obſervation. It is not to
be imagined, that letters written in the intimacy of Chriſ
tian friendſhip, ſome of them with the moſt apparent mark
of haſte, and amidſt a variety of important public cares
ſhould be adorned with any ſtudied elegance of expreſſion
about which the greatneſs of his ſoul would not allow him t
be at any time very ſolicitous; for he generally (ſo far as
could obſerve.) wrote as faſt as his pen could move, whic
happily both for him and his many friends, was very freely
Yet here the grandeur of his ſubjeċt has ſometimes clothe
his ideas with a language more elevated, than is ordinaril
to be expeċted in an epiſtolary correſpondence. The preſ
ſcorners, who may deride ſentiments and enjoyments lik
thoſe which this truly great man ſo experimentally and pa
thetically deſcribes I pity from my heart; and grieve
think, how unfit they muſt be for the hallelujahs of heaven
who pour contempt upon the neareſt approaches to them
Nor ſhall I think it any misfortu e, to ſhare with ſo exce
lent a perſon in their profane deriſion. It will be infinite
more than an equivalent for all that ſuch ignorance and p
tulancy can think and ſay, if I may convince ſome who a
as yet ſtrangers to religion, how real, and how noble, i
delights are; if I may engage my pious readers, to glori
God for ſo illuſtrious an inſtance of his grace; and finall
if I may quic .en them, and above all may rouſe my own t
indolent ſpirit, to follow with leſs unequal ſteps an exampl
to the ſublimity of which. I fear few of us ſhall after all
able fully to attain. And that we may not be too much d
couraged under the deficiency, let it be recollected, that fe
have the advantage of a temper naturally ſo warm; few ha
an equal command of retirement; and perhaps hardly a
one, who thinks himſelf moſt indebted to the riches and fre
dom of divine grace, can trace interpoſitions of it, in all
ſpeċts equally aſtoniſhing.

§. 53. The firſt of theſe extraordinary letters which ha
fallen into my hand, is dated near three years after his cc
verſion, and addreſſed to a lady of quality. I believe it
the firſt the Major ever wrote, ſo immediately on the ſu
ject of his religious conſolations and converſe with God
devout retirement. For I well remember, that he once t
me, he was ſo much afraid that ſomething of ſpiritual pr
ſhould mingle itſelf with the relation of ſuch kind of ex

·iences, that he concealed them a long time : but obferviug
with how much freedom the facred writers open all the moft
ecret receffes of their hearts, efpecially in the Pfalms, his
:onfcience began to be burthened, under an apprehenfion,
hat, for the honor of God, and in order to engage the con-
:urrent praifes of fome of his people, he ought to difclofe
hem. On this he fet himfelf to refleɛt, who among all his
1umerous acquaintance feemed at once the moft experienced
:hriftian he knew, (to whom therefore fuch things as he
1ad to communicate might appear folid and credible,) and
who the humbleſt. He quickly thought of the lady Mar-
:hionefs of Douglas, in this view : And the reader may
well imagine, that it ftruck my mind very ftrongly, to
hink that now, more than twenty-four years after it was
written, Providence fhould bring to my hand, (as it has
lone within thefe few days.) what I affuredly believe to be
1 genuine copy of that very letter ; which I had not the leaft
:eafon to expeɛt I fhould ever have feen, when I learnt
from his own mouth, amidft the freedom of an accidental
:onverfation, the occafion and circumftances of it.

§. 59. It is dated from London, July 21, 1722, and the
very firft lines of it relate to a remarkable circumftance,
which from others of his letters I find to have happened feveral times. I mean, that when he had received from any
of his chriftian friends a few lines which particularly affeɛt-
ed his heart, he could not ftay till the ftated return of his
devotional hour, but immediately retired to pray for them,
and to give vent to thofe religious emotions of mind which
fuch a correfpondence raifed. How invaluable was fuch a
friend ? And how great reafon have thofe of us, who once
poffeffed a large fhare in his heart, and in thofe retired and
facred moments. to blefs God for fo fingular a felicity ; and
to comfort ourfelves in a pleafing hope, that we may yet
reap future bleffings, as the harveft of thofe petitions which
he can no more repeat.

§. 60. His words are thefe: "I was fo happy as to re-
" ceive yours juft as I arrived, and I had no fooner read it,
" but ' fhut my door, and fought him whom my foul loveth.
" I fought him, and found him ; and would not let him go,
" till he had bleffed us all. It is impoffible to find words,
" to exprefs what I obtained ; but I fuppofe, it was fome-
" thing like that which the difciples got, as they were go-

" ing to Emmaus, when they said, did not our hearts burn
" within us, &c. or rather like what Paul felt, when he
" could not tell whether he was in the body, or out of it,"
He then mentions his dread of spiritual pride, from which
he earnestly prays that God may deliver and preserve him.
" This," says he, " would have hindered me from commu-
" nicating these things, if I had not such an example be-
" fore me, as the man after God's own heart, saying, I
" will declare what God hath done for my soul; and else-
" where, the humble shall hear thereof, and be glad: now
" I am well satisfied, that your ladyship is of that number."
He then adds, " I had no sooner finished this exercise,"
that is, of prayer abovementioned, " but I sat down to ad-
" mire the goodness of my God, that he would vouchsafe
" to influence by his free Spirit so undeserving a wretch as
" I, and to make me thus to mount up with eagles wings.
" And here I was lost again, and got into an ocean. where
" I could neither find bound nor bottom ; but was obliged to
" cry out with the apostle, Oh the breadth, the length, the
" depth, the height, of the love of Christ which passeth know-
" ledge! But if I give way to this strain, I shall never
" have done. That the God of hope may fill you with all
" joy and peace in believing, that you may abound in hope
" through the power of the Holy Ghost, shall always be the
" prayer of him, who is, with the greatest sincerity and
" respect, your ladyship's, &c."

§. 61. Another passage to the same purpose I find in a
memorandum, which he seems to have written for his own
use, dated Monday, March 11, which I perceive from many concurrent circumstances, must have been in the year
1722-3. " This day," says he, " having been to visit Mrs.
" G. at Hampstead, I came home about two, and read a
" sermon on those words, Psal. cxxx. 4. But there is for-
" giveness with thee, that thou mayest be feared : About the
" latter end of which, there is a description of the miserable
" condition of those that are slighters of pardoning grace.
" From a sense of the great obligations I lay under to the
" almighty God, who hath made me to differ from such,
" from what I was, and from the rest of my companions, I
" knelt down to praise his holy name; and I know not, that
" in my life time I ever lay lower in the dust, never having
" had a fuller view of my own unworthiness. I never plead-

" ed more ftro gly the merits and interceffion of him, who
" I know is worthy ; never vowed more fincerely to be
" the Lord's, and to accept of Chrift as he is offered in the
" gofpel, as my king, prieft, and prophet ; never had fo
" ftrong a defire to depart, that I might fin no more ; but
" ————my grace is fufficient——curbed that defire. I
" never pleaded with greater fervency for the Comforter,
" which, our bleffed Lord hath promifed, fhall abide with
" us for ever For all which I defire to afcribe glory, &c.
" to Him that fitteth on the throne, and to the Lamb."

§ 62. There are feveral others of his papers, which fpeak
much the fame language ; which, had he kept a diary, would
(I doubt not) have filled many fheets. I believe, my devout readers would not foon be weary of reading extracts of
this kind : But that I may not exceed in this part of my
narrative. I fhall mention only two more, each of them dated fome years after ; that is, one from Douglas, April 1,
1725; and the other from Stranrawen, the 25th of May
following.

§. 63. The former of thefe relates to the frame of his
fpirit on a journey. On the mention of which I cannot but
recollect, how often I have heard him fay, that fome of the
moft delightful days of his life were days in which he tra-
velled alone, (that is, with only a fervant at a diftance;)
when he could, efpecially in roads not much frequented,
indulge himfelf in the pleafures of prayer and praife. In
the exercife of which laft, he was greatly affifted by feveral
pfalms and hymns, which he had treafured up in his memory, and which he ufed not only to repeat aloud, but fometimes to fing. In reference to this I remember the following paffage, in a letter which he wrote to me many years
after, when on mentioning my ever dear and honored friend
the Rev. Dr Watts, he fays. " How often in finging fome
of his pfalms. hymns, or lyricks, on horfe-back, and elfewhere, has the evil fpirit been made to flee :

" When e'er my heart in tune was found',
" Like David's harp of folemn found !"

§. 64 Such was the firft of April above mentioned, in
the evening of which he writes thus to an intimate friend :
" What would I have given this day upon the road, for pa-
" per, pen, and ink, when the Spirit of the moft High

E

" reſted upon me ? Ch for the pen of a ready writer, and
" the tongue of an angel, to declare what God hath done
" this day for my. ſoul! But in ſhort, it is in vain to at-
" tempt it : All that I am able to ſay, is only this, that my
" ſoul has been for ſome hours joining with the bleſſed ſpi-
" rits above, in giving glory, and honor, and praiſe, unto
" Him that ſitteth upon the throne, and to the Lamb for e-
" ver and ever. My praiſes began from a renewed view
" of Him, whom I ſaw pierced for my tranſgreſſions. I
" ſummoned the whole hierarchy of heaven to join with me ;
" and I am perſuaded, they all echoed back praiſe to the
" moſt High. Yes, one would have thought, the very
" larks joined me with emulation. Sure then I need not
" make uſe of many words, to perſuade you that are his
" ſaints, to join me in bleſſing and praiſing his holy name,"·
He concludes, " May the bleſſing of the God of Jacob reſt
" upon you all ! Adieu. Written in great haſte, late and
" weary."

§ 65. Scarce can I here refrain from breaking out into
more copious reflections on the exquiſite pleaſures of true
religion, when riſen to ſuch eminent degrees ; which can
thus feaſt the ſoul in his ſolitude, and refreſh it on journeys ;
and bring down ſo much of heaven to earth, as this delightful letter expreſſes. But the remark is ſo obvious, that I
will not enlarge upon it ; but proceed to the other letter a-
bove mentioned, which was written the next month, on the
Tueſday after a ſacrament day,

§. 65.·He mentions the pleaſure with which he had attended a preparation ſermon the Saturday before ; and then
he adds, " I took a walk upon the mountains that are over
" againſt Ireland ; and I perſuade myſelf, that were I capa-
" ble of giving you a deſcription of what paſſed there, you
" would agree, that I had much better reaſon to remember
" my God from the hills of Port Patrick, than David from
" the land of Jordan, and of the Hermonites, from the hill
" Mizar." I ſuppoſe, he means, in reference to the clear-
er diſcoveries of the goſpel with which we are favored,
" In ſhort," ſays he immediately afterwards, in that ſcripture phraſe which was become ſo familiar to him, " I wreſt-
" led ſome hours with the Angel of the covenant, and made
" ſupplications to him with floods of tears and cries,———
" until I had almoſt expired : But he ſtrengthened me ſo,

" that like Jacob, I had power with God, and prevailed.
" This," adds he, " is but a very faint defcription : You
" will be more able to judge of it, by what you have felt
" yourfelf upon the like occafions. After fuch preparatory
" work, I need not tell you, how bleffed the folemn ordi-
" nance of the Lord's fupper proved to me ; I hope, it was
" fo to many. You may believe, I fhould have been exceed-
" ing glad, if my gracious Lord had ordered it fo, that I
" might have made you a vifit, as I propofed : But I am
" now glad it was ordered otherwife, fince he hath caufed fo
" much of his goodnefs to pafs before me. Were I to give
" you an account of the many favors my God hath loaded
" me with fince I parted from you, I muft have taken up
" many days in nothing but writing. I hope, you will join
" with me in praifes for all the goodnefs he has fhewn to
" your unworthy brother in the Lord."

§. 67. Such were the ardors and elevations of his foul :
But while I record thefe memorials of them, I am very fenfible, there are many who will be inclined to cenfure them,
as the flights of enthufiafm ; for which reafon I muft beg
leave to add a remark or two on the occafion, which will be
illuftrated by feveral other extracts, which I fhall introduce
into the fequel of thefe memoirs. The one is, that he never
pretends, in any of the paffages cited above, or elfewhere,
to have received any immediate revelations from God, which
fhould raife him above the ordinary methods of inftruction,
or difcover any thing to him, whether of doctrines or facts.
No man was farther from pretending to predict future events,
except it were from the moral prognoftications of caufes naturally tending to produce them ; in tracing of which he had
indeed an admirable fagacity, as I have feen in fome very
remarkable inftances. Neither was he at all inclinable to
govern himfelf by fecret impulfes upon his mind, leading
him to things for which he could affign no reafon but the
impulfe itfelf. Had he ventured, in a prefumption on fuch
fecret agitations of mind, to teach, or to do any thing, not
warranted by the dictates of found fenfe and the word of God,
I fhould readily have acknowledged him an enthufiaft ; unlefs he could have produced fome other evidence than his
own perfuafion, to have fupported the authority of them.
But thefe ardent expreffions, which fome may call enthufiafm, feem only to evidence a heart deeply affected with a

ſenſe of the divine preſence and perfections, and of that love which paſſeth knowledge; eſpecially, as manifeſted in our redemption by the Son of God, which did indeed inflame his whole ſoul. And he thought, he might reaſonably aſcribe theſe ſtrong impreſſions, to which men are generally ſuch ſtrangers, and of which he had long been entirely deſtitute to the agency or influence of the Spirit of God upon his heart; and that, in proportion to the degree in which he felt them, he might properly ſay, God was preſent with him, and he converſed with God.* Now when we conſider the ſcriptural phraſes, of walking with God, of having communion with the Father and his Son Jeſus Chriſt, of Chriſt's coming to them that open the door of their hearts to him, and ſupping with them, of God's ſhedding abroad his love in the heart by his Spirit, of his coming with Jeſus Chriſt and making his abode with any man that loves him, of his meeting him that worketh righteouſneſs, of his making us glad by the light of his countenance, and a variety of other equivalent expreſſions; I believe, we ſhall all ſee reaſon to judge much more favorably of ſuch expreſſions as thoſe now in queſtion, than perſons who are themſelves ſtrangers to elevated devotion, and perhaps converſe but little with their bible, are inclined to do; eſpecially if they have, as many ſuch perſons have, a temper that inclines them to cavil and find fault. And I muſt farther obſerve, that amidſt all theſe

---

* The ingenious and pious Mr. Grove, (who I think was as little ſuſpected of running into enthuſiaſtical extreams, as moſt divines I could name,) has a noble paſſage to this purpoſe, in the ſixth volume of his poſthumous works, page 40, 41, which reſpect to the memory of both theſe excellent perſons inclines me to inſert here. "How often are good thoughts ſuggeſted," (viz. to the pure in heart,) "Heavenly affections kindled, and "inflamed? How often is the chriſtian prompted to holy actions, "drawn to his duty, reſtored, quickened, perſuaded, in ſuch a "manner, that he would be unjuſt to the Spirit of God to queſ- "tion his agency in the whole? Yes, oh my ſoul, there is a "Supreme Being, who governs the world, and is preſent with "it, who takes up his more ſpecial habitation in good men, and "is nigh to all who call upon him, to ſanctify, and aſſiſt them! "Haſt thou not felt him, oh my ſoul, like another ſoul, actua- "ting thy faculties, exalting thy views, purifying thy paſſions, "exciting thy graces, and begetting in thee an abhorrence of "ſin, and a love of holineſs? And is not all this an argument of "his preſence, as truly as if thou didſt ſee him?"

freedoms, with which this eminent chriftian opens his devout heart to the moft intimate of his friends, he ftill fpeaks
with profound awe and reverence of his heavenly Father,
and his Saviour, and maintains (after the example of the
facred writers themfelves,) a kind of dignity in his expreffions, fuitable to fuch a fubject; without any of that fond
familiarity of language, and degrading meannefs of phrafe,
by which it is, efpecially of late, grown fafhionable among
fome, (who neverthelefs I believe mean well,) to exprefs
their love and their humility.

§. 68. On the whole; if habitual love to God, firm
faith in the Lord Jefus Chrift, a fteady dependance on the
divine promifes, a full perfuafion of the wifdom and goodnefs of all the difpenfations of providence, a high efteem for
the bleffings of the heavenly world, and a fincere contempt
for the vanities of this, can properly be called enthufiafm;
then was Colonel Gardiner indeed one of the greateft en-
thufiafts our age has produced; and in proportion to the degree in which he was fo, I muft efteem him one of the wif-
eft and happieft of mankind. Nor do I fear to tell the
world, that it is the defign of my writing thefe memoirs,
and of every thing elfe that I undertake in life, to fpread
this glorious and bleffed enthufiafm; which I know to be the
anticipation of heaven, as well as the moft certain way to it.

§. 69. But left any fhould poffibly imagine, that allow-
ing the experiences which have been defcribed above, to
have been ever fo folid and important, yet there may be
fome appearance of boafting in fo free a communication of
them; I muft add to what I have hinted in reference to this
above, that I find in many of the papers before me very
genuine expreffions of the deepeft humility and felf-abafe-
ment; which indeed fuch holy converfe with God in prayer and praife, does above all things in the world tend to infpire and promote. Thus in one of his letters he fays, " I
" am but as a beaft before him:" In another he calls himfelf "a miferable hell-deferving finner:" And in another
he cries out, " Oh how good a mafter do I ferve; but alas,
" how ungrateful am I! What can be fo aftonifhing, as the
" love of Chrift to us, unlefs it be the coldnefs of our finful
" hearts towards fuch a Saviour?" With many other claufes
of the like nature, which I fhall not fet myfelf more parti-

cularly to trace, through the variety of letters in which they occur.

§. 70 It is a farther instance of this unfeigned humility, that when (as his lady with her usual propriety of language expresses it, in one of her letters to me concerning him,) " these divine joys and consolations were not his daily al- " lowance," he with equal freedom, in the confidence of christian friendship, acknowledges and laments it. Thus in the first letter I had the honour of receiving from him, dated from Leicester, July 9 1739, when he had been mentioning the blessing with which it had pleased God to at- tend my last address to him, and the influence it had upon his mind, he adds, " Much do I stand in need of every " help, to awaken me out of that spiritual deadness, which " seizes me so often. Once indeed it was quite otherwise " with me, and that for many years :

" Firm was my health, my day was bright,
" And I presum'd 'twould ne'er be night :
" Fondly I said within my heart,
" Pleasure and peace shall ne'er depart.
" But I forgot, thine arm was strong,
" Which made my mountain stand so long :
" Soon as thy face began to hide,
" My health was gone, my comforts dy'd.

" And here," adds he, " lies my sin, and my folly."

§. 71. I mention this, that the whole matter may be seen just as it was, and that other christians may not be discou- raged, if they feel some abatement of that fervor, and of those holy joys, which they have experienced during some of the first months or years of their spiritual life. But with relation to the Colonel, I have great reason to believe, that these which he laments as his days of spiritual deadness were not unanimated ; and that quickly after the date of this let- ter, and especially, nearer the close of his life, he had far- ther revivings, as the joyful anticipation of those better things in reserve, which were then nearly approaching. And thus Mr. Spears, in the letter I mentioned above, tells us he related the matter to him ; (for he studies as much as possible to retain the Colonel's own words :) " However, says he, after that happy period of sensible

" communion, though my joys and enlargements were not
" fo overflowing and fenfible, yet I have had habitual real
" communion with God from that day to this;" the latter
end of the year 1743; "and I know myfelf, and all that
" know me fee, that through the grace of God, to which
" I afcribe all, my converfation has been becoming the gof-
" pel; and let me die, whenever it fhall pleafe God, or
" wherever it fhall be, I am fure, I fhall go to the manfions
" of eternal glory, &c." And this is perfectly agreeable to
the manner in which he ufed to fpeak to me on this head,
which we have talked over frequently and largely.

§. 72. In this connection I hope my reader will forgive
my inferting a little ftory, which I received from a very
worthy minifter in Scotland, and which I fhall give in his
own words. "In this period," meaning that which followed the firft feven years after his converfion, "when his
" complaint of comparative deadnefs and languor in religion
" began, he had a dream; which, though he had no turn
" at all for taking notice of dreams, yet made a very ftrong
" impreffion upon his mind. He imagined, that he faw
" his bleffed Redeemer on earth, and that he was follow-
" ing him through a large field. following him whom his
" foul loved but much troubled, becaufe he thought his
" bleffed Lord did not fpeak to him; till he came up to the
" gate of a burying-place, when turning about he fmil-
" ed upon him, in fuch a manner as filled his foul with the
" moft ravifhing joy; and on after reflection animated
" his faith, in believing that whatever ftorms and darknefs
" he might meet with in the way, at the hour of death his
" glorious Redeemer would lift upon him the light of his
" life-giving countenance." My correfpondent adds a circumftance, for which he maks fome apology, as what may
feem whimfical, and yet made fome impreffion on himfelf;
" that there was a remarkable refemblance in the field in
" which this brave man met death, and that he had repre-
" fented to him in the dream." I did not fully underftand
this at firft; but a paffage in that letter from Mr. pears,
which I have mentioned more than once, has cleared it.
" Now obferve, Sir, this feems to be a literal defcription
" of the place, where this chriftian hero ended his forrows
" and conflicts, and from which he entered triumphantly
" into the joy of his Lord. For after he fell in the battle,

" fighting gloriously for his king and the caufe of his God,
" his wounded body while life was yet remaining, was
" carried from the field of battle by the eaft fide of his own
" inclofure, till he came to the church yard of Tranent,
" and was brought to the minifter's houfe ; where he foon
" after breathed out his foul into the hands of his Lord,
" and was conducted to his prefence, where there is fulnefs
" of joy, without any cloud of interruption for ever."

§ 73. I well know, that in dreams there are diverfe
vanities, and readily acknowledge, that nothing certain
could be inferred from this : Yet it feems at leaft to fhew,
which way the imagination was working even in fleep ; and
I cannot think it unworthy of a wife and good man, fometimes to reflect with complacency on any images, which
paffing through his mind even in that ftate, may tend either
to exprefs, or to quicken, his love to the great Saviour.
Thofe eminently pious divines of the church of England,
bifhop Bull, and bifhop Ken, do both intimate it as their
opinion, that it may be a part of the fervice of miniftering
angels to fuggeft devout dreams : * And I know, that the
worthy perfon of whom I fpeak, was well acquainted with
that evening hymn of the latter of thofe excellent writers,
which has thefe lines :

   " Lord, left the tempter me furprize,
   " Watch over thine own facrifice !
   " All loofe, all idle thoughts caft out ;
   " And make my very dreams devout !"

Nor would it be difficult to produce other paffages much to the
fame purpofe, † if it would not be deemed too great a digreffion

* Bifhop Bull has thefe remarkable words " Although I am
" no doater on dreams, yet I verily belive, that fome dreams are
" monitory, above the power of fancy, and impreffed upon us by
" fome fuperior influence. For of fuch dreams we have plain
" and undeniable inftances in hiftory, both facred and profane,
" and in our own age and obfervation. Nor fhall I fo value the
" laughter of fcepticks, and the fcoffs of the epicureans, as to
" be afhamed to profefs, that I myfelf have had fome convincing
" experimen's of fuch impreffions." Bifhop Bull's ferm. and
difc Vol. II. pag. 489, 490.

† If I miftake not, the fame bifhop Ken is the author of a mid-
night hymn, concluding with thefe words :
   " May my ætherial Guardian kindly fpread ·
   " His wings, and from the tempter fcreen my head ;

from our fubject, and too laboured a vindication of a
little incident, of very fmall importance, when compared
with moft of thofe which make up this narrative.

§. 74. I meet not with any other remarkable event relating to Major Gardiner, which can properly be introduced here, till the year 1726; when, on the 11th day of July, he was married to the right hon. the lady Frances Er-
fkine, daughter to the late Earl of Buchan, by whom he
had thirteen children, five only of which furvived their father, two fons, and three daughters: whom I cannot mention without the moft fervent prayers to God for them, that
they may always behave worthy the honour of being de-
fcended from fuch parents; and that the God of their father, and of their mother, may make them perpetually the
care of his providence, and yet more eminently happy in
the conftant and abundant influences of his grace!

§. 75. As her ladyfhip is ftill living, (and for the fake
of her dear offspring, and numerous friends, may fhe long
be fpared!) I fhall not here indulge myfelf in faying any
thing of her; except it be, that the Colonel affured me,
when he had been happy in this intimate relation to her more
than fourteen years; that the greateft imperfection he knew
in her character was, " that fhe valued and loved him much
" more than he deferved." And little did he think, in the
fimplicity of heart with which he fpoke this how high an
encomium he was making upon her, and how lafting an honor fuch a teftimony muft leave upon her name, long as the
memory of it fhall continue.

§ 76. As I do not intend in thefe memoirs a laboured
effay on the character of Colonel Gardiner, digefted under
the various virtues and graces which chriftianity requires,
(which would, I think, be a little too formal for a work of
this kind. and would give it fuch an air of panegyrick, as
would neither fuit my defign, nor be at all likely to render

" Grant of celeftial light fome piercing beams,
" To blefs my fleep, and fanctify my dreams!"
As he certainly was of thofe exactly parallel lines:
    " Oh may my Guardian, while I fleep,
    " Clofe to my bed his vigils keep:
    " His love angelical diftill,
    " To ftop the avenues of ill!
    " May he celeftial joys rehearfe,
    " And thought to thought with me converfe!"

it more uſeful;) I ſhall now mention what I have either obſerved in him, or heard concerning him, with regard to
thoſe domeſtic relations, which commenced about this time,
or quickly after. And here my reader will eaſily conclude,
that the reſolution of Joſhua was from the firſt adopted and
declared, " As for me, and my houſe, we will ſerve the
" Lord." It will naturally be ſuppoſed, that as ſoon as he
had a houſe, he erected an altar in it ; that the word of
God was read there, and prayers and praiſes were conſtant-
ly offered. Theſe were not to be omitted, on account of
any gueſt ; for he eſteemed it a part of due reſpect to thoſe
that remained under his roof, to take it for granted, they
would look upon it as a very bad compliment, to imagine
they would have been obliged, by neglecting the duties of
religion on their account. As his family increaſed, he had
a miniſter ſtatedly reſident in his houſe, who both diſcharg-
ed the office of a tutor to his children, and of a chaplain ;
and who was always treated with a becoming kindneſs and
reſpect. But in his abſence, the Colonel himſelf led the
devotions of the family ; and they were happy, who had an
opportunity of knowing, with how much ſolemnity, fervor,
and propriety, he did it.

§. 77. He was conſtant in attending upon public worſhip,
in which an exemplary care was taken, that the children
and ſervants might accompany the heads of the family. And
how he would have reſented the non attendance of any
member of it, may eaſily be conjectured, from a free, but
lively paſſage, in a letter to one of his intimate friends, on
an occaſion which it is not material to mention. " Oh,
" Sir, had a child of yours under my roof but once ne-
" glected the public worſhip of God, when he was able to
" attend it, I ſhould have been ready to conclude he had
" been diſtracted; and ſhould have thought of ſhaving his
" head, and confining him in a dark room."

§. 78. He always treated his lady with a manly tenderneſs,
giving her the moſt natural evidences of a cordial habitual e-
ſteem, and expreſſing a moſt affectionate ſympathy with
her, under the infirmities of a very delicate conſtitution,
much broken, at leaſt towards the latter years of their marriage, in conſequence of ſo frequent pregnancy. He had at
all times a moſt faithful care of all her intereſts, and eſpecially thoſe relating to the ſtate of religion in her mind,

His converfation, and his letters, concurred to cherifh thofe fublime ideas, which chriftianity fuggefts;. to promote our fubmiffion to the will of God, to teach us to center our happinefs in the great Author of our being, and to live by faith in the invifible world. Thefe, no doubt, were frequently the fubjeds of mutual difcourfe : And many letters, which her ladyfhip has had the goodnefs to communicate to me, are moft convincing evidences of the degree in which this noble and moft friendly care filled his mind in the days of their feparation ; days, which fo entire a mutual affection muft have rendered exceeding painful, had they not been fupported by fuch exalted fentiments of piety, and fweetened by daily communion with an ever prefent and ever gracious God.

§. 79. The neceffity of being fo many months together diftant from his family, hindered him from many of thofe condefcending labours in cultivating the minds of his children in early life, which to a foul fo benevolent, fo wife, and fo zealous, would undoubtedly have afforded a very exquifite pleafure. The care of his worthy confort, who well knew, that it is one of the brighteft parts of a mother's character, and one of the moft important views in which the fex can be confidered, made him the eafier under fuch a circumftance : But when he was with them, he failed not to inftruct and admonifh them ; and the conftant deep fenfe with which he fpoke of divine things, and the real unaffected indifference which he always fhewed for what this vain world is moft ready to admire, were excellent leffons of daily wifdom, which I hope they will recollect with advantage in every future fcene of life. And I have feen fuch hints in his letters relating to them, as plainly fhew with how great a weight they lay on his mind, and how highly he defired above all things that they might be the faithful difciples of Chrift, and acquainted betimes with the unequalled pleafures and bleffings of religion. He thought an excefs of delicacy, and of indulgence, one of the moft dangerous faults in education, by which he every where faw great numbers of young people undone : Yet he was folicitous to guard againft a feverity, which might terrify or difcourage ; and though he endeavoured to take all prudent precautions to prevent the commiffion of faults, yet when they had been committed, and there feemed to be a fenfe of them, he was always ready to make the moſt candid allowances for the thoughtlefsnefs of unripened years, and tenderly to cheriſh every purpofe of a more proper conduct for the time to come.

§. 80. It was eafy to perceive, that the openings of genius in the young branches of his family gave him great delight, and that he had a fecret ambition to fee them excel in what they undertook Yet he was greatly cautious over his heart, leſt it ſhould be too fondly attached to them ; and as he was one of the moſt eminent proficients I ever knew, in the bleſſed fcience of refignation to the divine will, fo there was no effect of that refignation which appeared to me more admirable, than what related to the life of his children. An experience, which no length of time will ever efface out of my memory, has fo fenfibly taught me, how difficult it is fully to fupport the chriſtian character here, that I hope my reader will pardon me, (I am fure at leaſt the heart of wounded parents will,) if I dwell a little longer upon fo intereſting a fubject.

§ 81. When he was in Herefordſhire, in the month of July, in the year 1734, it pleafed God to vifit his little family with the fmall-pox. Five days before the date of the letter I am juſt going to mention, he had received the agreeble news, that there was a profpect of the recovery of his fon, then under that awful vifitation ; and he had been expreffing his thankfulnefs for it, in a letter which he had fent away but a few hours before he was informed of his death ; the furprize of which in this connection, muſt naturally be very great. But behold (fays the reverend and worthy perfon from whom I received the copy his truly filial fubmiffion to the will of his heavenly Father, in the following lines addreſſed to the dear partner of his affliction:

" Your refignation to the will of God under this difpenfa-
" tion, gives me more joy, than the death of the child has
" given me forrow. He, to be fure, is happy ; and we
" ſhall go to him, though he ſhall not return to us.
" Oh that we had our latter end always in view !—We ſhall
" foon follow ; and oh what reafon have we to long for that
" glorious day, when we ſhall get quit of this body of fin
" and death, under which we now groan, and which ren-
" ders this life fo wretched ! I defire to blefs God, that—
" [another of his children] is in fo good a way : But I have

" refigned her. We muft not choofe for ourfelves; and it
" is well we muft not, for we fhould often make a very bad
" choice. And therefore it is our wifdom, as well as our
" duty, to leave all with a gracious God; who hath promi-
" fed, that all things fhall work together for good to thofe
" that love him: and he is faithful that hath promifed, who
" will infallibly perform it, if our unbelief does not ftand in
" the way."

§. 82. The greateft trial of this kind that he ever bore,
was in the removal of his fecond fon, who was one of the
moft amiable and promifing children that has been known.
The dear little creature was the darling of all that knew him,
and promifed very fair, fo far as a child could be known by
its doings, to have been a great ornament to the family, and
bleffing to the public. The fuddennefs of the ftroke muft,
no doubt, render it the more painful; for this beloved child
was fnatched away by an illnefs, which feized him but about
fifteen hours before it carried him off. He died in the month
of October, 1733, at near fix years old. Their friends were
ready to fear, that his affectionate parents would be almoft
overwhelmed with fuch a lofs: but the happy father had fo
firm a perfuafion, that God had received the dear little one
to the felicities of the celeftial world; and at the fame time
had fo ftrong a fenfe of the divine goodnefs, in taking one
of his children, and that too one who lay fo near his heart,
fo early to himfelf; that the forrows of nature were quite
fwallowed up in the fublime joy which thefe confiderations
adminiftered. When he reflected, what human life is;
how many its fnares and temptations are; and how frequently children, who once promifed very well, are infenfibly
corrupted, and at length undone; with Solomon, he bleffed the dead already dead, more than the living who were
yet alive, and felt an unfpeakable pleafure, in looking after
the lovely infant, as fafely and delightfully lodged in the
houfe of its heavenly Father. Yea, he affured me, that his
heart was at this time fo entirely taken up with thefe views,
that he was afraid, they who did not thoroughly know him,
might fufpect, that he was deficient in the natural affections
of a parent; while thus borne above the anguifh of them,
by the views which faith adminiftered to him, and which
divine grace fupported in his foul.

F

§. 83. So much did he, on one of the moſt trying occaſions of life, manifeſt of the temper of a glorified ſaint; and
to ſuch happy purpoſes did he retain thoſe leſſons of ſubmiſſion to God, and acquieſcence in him, which I remember
he once inculcated in a letter he wrote to a lady of quality,
under the apprehenſion of a breach in her family, with which
Providence ſeemed to threaten her; which I am willing to inſert here, though a little out of what might ſeem
its proper place, rather than entirely to omit it.   It is dated
from London, June 16, 1722, when ſpeaking of the dangerous illneſs of a dear relative, he has theſe words : " When
" my mind runs hither," that is, to God, as its refuge
and ſtrong defence, (as the connection plainly determines
it,) " I think I can bear any thing, the loſs of all, the loſs
" of health, of relations on whom I depend, and whom
" I love, all that is dear to me, without repining or mur-
" muring.   When I think, that God orders, diſpoſes, and
" manages all things, according to the counſel of his own
" will ; when I think of the extent of his providence, that
" it reaches to the minuteſt things; then, though a uſeful
" friend or dear relative to be ſnatched away by death, I
" recall myſelf, and check my thoughts with theſe conſider-
" ations.   Is he not God, from everlaſting, and to ever-
" laſting ? And has he not promiſed to be a God to me ? A
" God in all his attributes, a God in all his perſons, a God
" in all his creatures, and providences ? And ſhall I dare
" to ſay, What ſhall I do ? Was he not the infinite cauſe
" of all I met with in the creatures ? And were not they
" the finite effects of his infinite love and kindneſs ? I have
" daily experienced, that the inſtrument was, and is, what
" God makes it to be ; and I know, that this God hath
" the hearts of all men in his hands, and the earth is the
" Lord's, and the fulneſs thereof. If this earth be good
" for me, I ſhall have it ; for my Father hath it all in poſ-
" ſeſſion. If favor in the eyes of men be good for me, I
" ſhall have it ; for the ſpring of every motion in the heart
" of man is in God's hand. My dear — ſeems now to be dy-
" ing ; but God is all wiſe. and every thing is done by him
" for the beſt. Shall I hold back any thing that is his own,
" when he requires it ? No, God forbid ! When I conſider
" the excellency of his glorious attributes, I am ſatisfied
" with all his dealings." I perceive by the introduction,

and by what follows, that moft, if not all of this, is a quotation from fomething written by a lady ; but whether from fome manufcript, or a printed book; whether exactly tranfcribed, or quoted from memory, I cannot determine : And therefore I thought proper to infert it, as the major (for that was the office he bore then,) by thus interweaving it with his letter makes it his own ; and as it feems to exprefs in a very lively manner the principles which bore him on, to a conduct fo truly great and heroic, in circumftances that have overwhelmed many an heart, that could have faced danger and death with the greateft intrepidity.

§. 84 I return now to confider his character in the domeftic relation of a mafter, on which I fhall not enlarge. It is however proper to remark, that as his habitual meeknefs, and command of his paffions, prevented indecent fallies of ungoverned anger towards thofe in the loweft ftate of fubjection to him, (by which fome in high life do ftrangely debafe themfelves, and lofe much of their authority,) fo the natural greatnefs of his mind made him folicitous to render their inferior ftations as eafy as he could ; and fo much the rather, becaufe he confidered all the children of Adam as ftanding upon a level before their great Creator, and had alfo a deeper fenfe of the dignity and worth of every immortal foul, how meanly foever it might chance to be lodged, than moft perfons I have known. This engaged him to give his fervants frequent religious exhortations and inftructions, as I have been affured by feveral who were fo happy as to live with him under that character. One of the firft letters after he entered on his chriftian coarfe, exprefles the fame difpofition ; in which with great tendernefs he recommends a fervant, who was in a bad ftate of health, to his mother's care, as he was well acquainted with her condefcending temper ; mentioning at the fame time the endeavors he had ufed, to promote his preparations for a better world, under an apprehenfion that he would not continue long in this. And we fhall have an affecting inftance of the prevalency of the fame difpofition, in the clofing fcene of his life, and indeed in the laft words he ever fpoke, which exprefled his generous folicitude for the fafety of a faithful fervant, who was then near him,

§. 84. As it was a few years after his marriage that he was promoted to the rank of lieutenant-colonel, in which he

continued till he had a regiment of his own ; I shall for the
future speak of him by that title ; and may not perhaps find
any more proper place, in which to mention, what it is proper for me to say of his behaviour and conduct as an officer.
I shall not here enlarge on his bravery in the field, though
that was very remarkable, as I have heard from others : I
say, from others, for I never heard any thing of that kind
from himself, nor knew, till after his death, that he was
present at almost every battle that was fought in Flanders,
while the illustrious Duke of Marlborough commanded the
allied army there.   I have also been assured · from several
very credible persons, some of whom were eye-witnesses,
that at the skirmish with the rebels at Preston in Lanca-
shire, (thirty years before that engagement at the other Preston, which deprived us of this gallant guardian of his country,) he signalized himself very particulaly : For he headed
a little body of men, I think about twelve, and set fire to
the barricado of the rebels in the face of their whole army,
while they were pouring in their shot, by which eight of the
twelve that attended him fell.   This was the last action of
the kind in which he was engaged, before the long peace
which ensued : And who can express, how happy it was
for him, and indeed for his country, of which he was ever
so generous, and in his latter years so important a friend,
that he did not fall then ; when the profaneness which mingled itself with his martial rage, seemed to rend the heavens,
and shocked some other military gentlemen, who were not
themselves remarkable for their caution in this respect.

§. 86. But I insist not on things of this nature, which the
true greatness of his soul would hardly ever permit him to
mention, unless, when it tended to illustrate the divine care
over him in these extremities of danger, and the grace of God
in calling him from so abandoned a state. It is well known, that
the character of an officer is not only to be approved in the
day of combat. Colonel Gardiner was truly sensible, that every
day brought its duties along with it ; and he was constantly
careful, that no pretence of amusement, friendship, or even
devotion itself, might prevent their being discharged in their
season.

§. 87, I doubt not, but the noble persons in whose regiment he was lieutenant colonel, will always be ready to
bear an honourable and grateful testimony to his exemplary di-

ligence and fidelity, in all that related to the care of the troops over which he was fet; whether with regard to the men, or the horfes. He knew, that it is incumbent on thofe who have the honour of prefiding over others, whether in civil, ecclefiaftical, or military offices, not to content themfelves with doing only fo much as may preferve them from the reproach of grofs and vifible neglect; but ferioufly to confider, how much they can poffibly do, without going out of their proper fphere, to ferve the public, by the due infpection of thofe committed to their care. The duties of the clofet, and of the fanctuary, were fo adjufted, as not to interfere with thofe of the parade, or any other place where the welfare of the regiment called him. On the other hand, he was folicitous, not to fuffer thefe things to interfere with religion; a due attendance to which he apprehended to be the fureft. method of attaining all defirable fuccefs in every other intereft and concern in life. He therefore abhorred every thing, that fhould look like a contrivance to keep his foldiers employed about their horfes and their arms at the feafons of public worfhip; (an indecency, which I wifh there was no room to mention:) Far from that, he ufed to have them drawn up juft before it began, and from the parade they went off to the houfe of God. He underftood the rights of confcience too well, to impofe his own particular profeffion in religion on others, or to ufe thofe who differed from him in the choice of its modes, the lefs kindly or refpectfully on that account. But as moft of his own company, and many of the reft, chofe (when in England,) to attend him to the diffenting chapel, he ufed to march them thither in due time, fo as to be there before worfhip began. And I muft do them the juftice to fay, that fo far as I could ever difcern, when I have feen them in large numbers before me, they behaved with as much reverence, gravity, and decorum, during the time of divine fervice, as any of their fellow worfhippers.

§ 88 That his remarkable care to maintain good difcipline among them (of which we fhall afterwards fpeak,) might be the more effectual, he made himfelf on all proper occafions acceffible to them, and expreffed a great concern for their intereft; which being fo genuine and fincere, naturally difcovered itfelf in a variety of inftances I remember, I had once occafion to vifit one of his dragoons, in his laſt illneſs, at Harborough, and I found the man upon the borders of eternity; a circumſtance, which, as he apprehended it himſelf, muſt add ſome peculiar weight and credibility to his diſcourſe.   And he then told me, in his colonel's abſence, that he queſtioned not, but he ſhould have everlaſting reaſon to bleſs God on Colonel Gardiner's account, for he had been a father to him in all his intereſts, both temporal and ſpiritual.   He added, that he had viſited him almoſt every day during his illneſs, with religious advice and inſtruction, as well as taken care that he ſhould want nothing, that might conduce to the recovery of his health.   And he did not ſpeak of this, as the reſult of any particular attachment to him, but as the manner in which he was accuſtomed to treat thoſe under his command.   It is no wonder, that this engaged their affection to a very great degree.   And I doubt not, that if he had fought the fatal battle of Preſton-Pans at the head of that gallant regiment, of which he had the care for ſo many years, and which is allowed by moſt unexceptionable judges to be one of the fineſt in the Britiſh ſervice, and conſequently in the world, he had been ſupported in a much different manner; and had found a much greater number, who would have rejoiced in an opportunity of making their own breaſts a barrier in the defence of his.

§. 89. It could not but greatly endear him to his ſoldiers, that ſo far as preferments lay in his power, or were under his influence, they were diſtributed according to merit; which he knew to be as much the dictate of prudence, as of equity.   I find by one of his letters before me, dated a few months before his happy change, that he was ſolicited to improve his intereſt with the Earl of Stair, in favour of one whom he judged a very worthy perſon; and that he had been ſuggeſted by another who recommended him, that if he ſucceeded he might expect ſome handſome acknowledgment.   But he anſwers with ſome degree of indignation; "Do you "imagine, I am bribed to do juſtice?" For ſuch it ſeems he eſteemed it, to confer the favour which was aſked from him, on one ſo deſerving.   Nothing can more effectually tend to humble the enemies of a ſtate, than that ſuch maxims ſhould univerſally prevail in it: And if they do not prevail, the worthieſt men in an army or fleet may be ſunk under repeated difcouragements, and the bafeft exalted, to the infamy of the public, and perhaps to its ruin.

§ 90. In the midft of all the gentlenefs which Colonel Gardiner exercifed towards his foldiers, he made it very apparent, that he knew how to reconcile the tendernefs of a real, faithful, and condefcending friend, with the authority of a commander. Perhaps hardly any thing conduced more generally to the maintaining of this authority, than the ftrict decorum: and good manners, with which he treated even the private gentlemen of his regiment ; which has always a great efficacy towards keeping inferiors at a proper diftance, and forbids, in the leaft offenfive manner, familiarities, which degrade the fuperior, and enervate his influence. The calmnefs and fteadinefs of his behaviour on all occafions, did alfo greatly tend to the fame purpofe. He knew, how mean a man looks in the tranfports of paffion, and would not ufe fo much freedom with any of his men, as to fall into fuch tranfports before them ; well knowing, that perfons in the loweft rank of life are aware, how unfit they are to govern others, who cannot govern themfelves. He was alfo fenfible, how neceffary it is in all who prefide over others, and efpecially in military officers, to check irregularities, when they firft begin to appear : And that he might be able to do it, he kept a ftrict infpection over his foldiers ; in which view it was obferved, that as he generally chofe to refide among them as much as he could, (though in circumftances which fometimes occafioned him to deny himfelf in fome interefts which were very dear to him,) fo when they were around him, he feldom ftaid long in a place : but was frequently walking the ftreets, and looking into their quarters and ftables, as well as reviewing and exercifing them himfelf. It has often been obferved, that the regiment of which he was fo many years lieutenant colonel, was one of the moft regular and orderly regiments in the public fervice ; fo that perhaps none of our dragoons were more welcome than they, to the towns where their character was known. Yet no fuch bodies of men are fo blamelefs in their conduct, but fomething will be found, efpecially among fuch confiderable numbers, worthy of cenfure, and fometimes of punifhment. This Colonel Gardiner knew how to inflict with a becoming refolution, and with all the feverity which he judged neceffary : A feverity the more awful and imprefling, as it was always attended with meeknefs; for he well knew, that when things are done in a paſſion, it feems only an accidental circumſtance that they are acts of juſtice, and that fuch indecencies greatly obſtruct the ends of puniſhment, both as it relates to reforming offenders, and to deterring others from an imitation of their faults.

§. 91. One inſtance of his conduct, which happened at Leiceſter, and was related by the perſon chiefly concerned to a worthy friend from whom I had it, I cannot forbear inferting. While part of the regiment was encamped in the neighbourhood of that place, the colonel went incognito to the camp in the middle of the night; for he fometimes lodged at his quarters in the town. One of the centinels then on duty had abandoned his poſt, and on being feized broke out into fome oaths, and profane execrations againſt thofe that difcovered him; a crime, of which the colonel had the greateſt abhorrence, and on which he never failed to animadvert. The man afterwards appeared much aſhamed, and concerned for what he had done. But the colonel ordered him to be brought early the next morning to his own quarters, where he had prepared a piquet, on which he appointed him a private fort of penance: And while he was put upon it, he difcourfed with him ferioufly and tenderly upon the evils and aggravations of his fault; admoniſhed him of the divine difpleafure which he had incurred; and urged him to argue from the pain which he then felt, how infinitely more dreadful it muſt be, to fall into the hands of the living God, and indeed to meet the terrors of that damnation, which he had been accuſtomed impioufly to call for on himfelf and his companions. The refult of this proceeding was, that the offender accepted his puniſhment, not only with fubmiſſion, but with thankfulnefs. He went away with a more cordial affection for his colonel, than he ever had before; and fpoke of it fome years after to my friend, in fuch a manner, that there feemed reafon to hope, it had been inſtrumental in producing, not only a change in his life, but in his heart.

§. 92. There cannot, I think, be a more proper place for mentioning the great reverence this excellent officer always expreſſed for the name of the bleſſed God, and the zeal with which he endeavoured to fupprefs, and if poſſible to extirpate, that deteſtable fin of fwearing and curfing,

which is every where fo common, and efpecially among
our military men. He often declared his fentiments with
refpect to this enormity, at the head of his regiment; and
urged his captains and their fubalterns, to take the greatest
care, that they did not give the fanction of their example,
to that which by their office they were obliged to punish in
others. And indeed his zeal on thefe eccasions wrought in
a very active, and fometimes in a remarkably fuccefsful
manner, not only among his equals, but fometimes among
his fuperiors too. An inftance of this in Flanders, I fhall
have an opportunity hereafter to produce; at prefent I fhall
only mention his conduct in Scotland a little before his death,
as I have it from a very valuable young minifter of that
country, on whofe teftimony I can thoroughly depend; and
I wifh, it may excite many to imitation.

§. 93. The commanding officer of the king's forces then
about Edinburgh, with the other colonels, and feveral other
gentlemen of rank in their refpective regiments, favoured
him with their company at Bankton, and took a dinner with
him. He too well ferefaw what might happen, amidft fuch
a variety of tempers and characters: and fearing, left his
confcience might have been enfnared by a finful filence, or
that on the other hand he might feem to pafs the bounds of
decency, and infringe upon the laws of hofpitality, by ani-
madverting on guefts fo juftly intitled to his regard; he happily determined on the following method of avoiding each
of thefe difficulties. As foon as they were come together,
he addreffed them with a great deal of refpect, and yet at
the fame time with a very frank and determined air; and
told them, that he had the honour in that diftrict to be a
juftice of the peace, and confequently that he was fworn to
put the laws in execution, and among the reft thofe againft
fwearing: That he could not execute them upon others
with any confidence, or by any means approve himfelf as a
man of impartiality and integrity to his own heart, if he
fuffered them to be broken in his prefence by perfons of any
rank whatfoever: And that therefore he intreated all the
gentlemen who then honoured him with their company,
that they would pleafe to be upon their guard; and that if
any oath or curfe fhould efcape them, he hoped they would
confider his legal animadverfion upon it, as a regard to the
duties of his office and the dictates of his confcience, and

not as owing to any want of deference to them. The commanding officer immediately ſupported him in this declaration, as entirely becoming the ſtation in which he was,
aſſuring him, that he would be ready to pay the penalty, if
he inadvertently tranſgreſſed ; and when Colonel Gardiner
on any occaſion ſtepped out of the room, he himſelf undertook to be the guardian of the law in his abſenſce ; and as
one of the inferior officers offended during this time, he informed the colonel, ſo that the fine was exacted, and given
to the poor, * with the univerſal approbation of the company. The ſtory ſpread in the neighbourhood, and was perhaps applauded highly by many, who wanted the courage
to go and do likewiſe. But it may be ſaid of the worthy
perſon of whom I write, with the utmoſt propriety, that
he feared the face of no man living where the honour of
God was concerned. In all ſuch caſes he might be juſtly
ſaid, in ſcripture phraſe, to ſet his face like a flint ; and I
aſſuredly believe, that had he been in the preſence of a ſovereign prince, who had been guilty of this fault, his looks
at leaſt would have teſtified his grief and ſurprize ; if he had
apprehended it unfit to have borne his teſtimony any other
way.

§. 94. Lord Codogan's regiment of dragoons during the
years I have mentioned, while he was lieutenant colonel of
it, was quartered in a great variety of places, both in England and Scotland, from many of which I have letters before me ; particularly, from Hamilton, Air, Carliſle,
Hereford, Maidenhead, Leiceſter, Warwick, Coventry,
Stamford, Harb rough, Northampton, and ſeveral other
places, eſpecially in our inland parts. The natural conſequence was, that the colonel, whoſe character was on many
accounts ſo very remarkable had a very extenſive acquaintance : And I believe I may certainly ſay, that wherever
he was known by perſons of wiſdom and worth, he was
proportionably reſpected, and left behind him traces of un-

---

* It is obſervable, that the money, which was forfeited on
this account by his own officers, whom he never ſpared, or by
any others of his ſoldiers, who rather choſe to pay them than to
ſubmit to corporal puniſhment, was by the colonel's order laid by
in bank, till ſome of the private men fell ſick ; and then it was
laid out, in providing them with proper help and accommodations
in their diſtreſs.

affected devotion, humility, benevolence, and zeal for the support and advancement of religion and virtue.

§. 95. The equable tenor of his mind in thefe refpects, is illuftrated by his letters from feveral of thefe places ; and though it is but comparatively a fmall number of them which I have now in my hands, yet they will afford fome valuable extracts ; which I fhall therefore here lay before my reader, that he may the better judge as to his real character, in particulars of which I have already difcourfed, or which may hereafter occur.

§, 96. In a letter to his lady, dated from Carlifle, Nov. 19, 1733, when he was on his journey to Herefordfhire, he breathes out his greatful chearful foul in thefe words :
" I blefs God, I was never better in my life time ; and I
" wifh I could be fo happy, as to hear the fame of you ;
" rather, (in other words,) to hear that you had obtained
" an entire truft in God.   That would infallibly keep you
" in perfect peace ; for the God of truth hath promifed it.
" Oh, how ought we to be longing to be with Chrift, which
" is infinitely better than any thing we can propofe here !
" To be there, where all complaints fhall be for ever ba-
" nifhed ; where no mountains fhall feparate between God
" and our fouls : And I hope, it will be fome addition to
" our happinefs, that you and I fhall be feparated no more ;
" but that as we have joined in finging the praifes of our
" glorious Redeemer here, we fhall fing them in a much
" higher key through an endlefs eternity   Oh eternity,
" eternity ! What a wonderful thought is eternity !"

§. 97. From Leicefter, Aug. 6, 17 9. he writes thus to this lady : " Yefterday I was at the Lords's table, where
" you and the children were not forgotten : But how won-
" derfully was I affifted when I came home, to plead for
" you all with many tears !" And then, fpeaking of fome intimate friends, who were impatient (as I fuppofe by the connection,) for his return to them, he takes occafion to obferve the necefhty " of endeavouring to compofe our
" minds, and to fay with the Pfalmift, my foul, wait thou
" only upon God." Afterwards, fpeaking of one of his children, of whom he heard that he made a commendable progrefs in learning, he expreffes his fatisfaction in it, and adds, " But how much greater joy would it give me. to hear
" that he was greatly advanced in the fchool of Chrift ?

" Oh that our children may but be wife to falvation; and
" may grow in grace, as they do in ftature!"

§. 98 Thefe letters, which to fo familiar a friend evidently lay open the heart, and fhew the ideas and affections which were lodged deepeft there, are fometimes taken up with an account of fermons he had attended, and the impreffion they had made upon his mind   I fhall mention one only, as a fpecimen of many more, which was dated from a place called Cohorn, April 15 " We had here a mini-
" fter from Wales, who gave us two excellent difcourfes
" on the love of Chrift to us, as an argument to engage
" our love to him.   And indeed, next to the greatnefs of
" his love to us, methinks there is nothing fo aftonifhing
" as the coldnefs of our love to him, Oh that he would
" fhed abroad his love upon our hearts by his holy Spirit,
" that ours might be kindled into a flame! May God ena-
" ble you to truft in him, and then you will be kept in per-
" fect peace!"

§. 99. We have met with many traces of that habitual gratitude to the bleffed God, as his heavenly Father and conftant friend, which made his life probably one of the happieft that ever was fpent on earth, I cannot omit one more, which appears to me the more worthy of notice, as being a fhort turn in as hafty a letter as any I remember to have feen of his, which he wrote from Leicefter, in June, 1739. " I am now under the deepeft fenfe of the many fa-
" vours the Almighty has beftowed upon me : Surely you
" will help me to celebrate the praifes of our gracious God
" and kind benefactor."   This exuberance of grateful affection, which, while it was almoft every hour pouring itfelf forth before God in the moft genuine and emphatical language, felt itfelf ftill as it were ftraitened for want of a fufficient vent, and therefore called on others to help him with their concurrent praifes, appears to me the moft glorious and happy ftate in which a human foul can find itfelf on this fide heaven.

§. 100. Such was the temper, which this excellent man appears to have carried along with him through fuch a variety of places and circumftances ; and the whole of his deportment was fuitable to thefe impreffions. Strangers were agreeably ftruck with his firft appearance, there was fo much of the chriftian, the well-bred man, and the univerfal friend in it; and as they came more intimately to know him, they difcovered, more and more, the uniformity and confiſtency of his whole temper and behaviour: ſo that whether he made only a viſit for a few days to any place, or continued there for many weeks or months, he was always beloved and e- ſteemed, and ſpoken of with that honorable teſtimony from perſons of the moſt different denominations and parties, which nothing but true ſterling worth, (if I may be allowed the expreſſion) and that in an eminent degree, can ſecure.

§. 101. Of the juſtice of this teſtimony, which I had ſo often heard from a variety of perſons, I myſelf began to be a witneſs about the time when the laſt mentioned letter was dated. In this view I believe I ſhall never forget that hap- py day, June 13, 1739, when I firſt met him at Leiceſter. I remember, I happened that day to preach a lecture from Pſal. cxix. 158. "I beheld the tranſgreſſors, and was grieved, " becauſe they kept not thy law." I was large in deſcribing that mixture of indignation and grief, (ſtrongly expreſſed by the original word there,) with which the good man looks on the daring tranſgreſſors of the divine law; and in tracing the cauſes of that grief, as ariſing from a regard to the di- vine honour, and the intereſt of a Redeemer, and a compaſ- ſionate concern for the miſery ſuch offenders bring on themſelves, and for the miſchief they do to the world about them. I little thought, how exactly I was drawing Colo- nel Gardiner's character under each of thoſe heads; and I have often reflected upon it as a happy providence, which opened a much ſpeedier way than I could have expected, to the breaſt of one of the moſt amiable and uſeful friends, which I ever expect to find upon earth. We afterwards ſung a hymn, which brought over again ſome of the leading thoughts in the ſermon, and ſtruck him ſo ſtrongly, that on obtaining a copy of it, he committed it to his memory, and uſed to repeat it with ſo forcible an accent, as ſhewed how much every line expreſſed of his very ſoul. In this view the reader will pardon my inſerting it; eſpecially, as I know not when I may get time to publiſh a volume of theſe ſerious, though artleſs compoſures, which I ſent him in manuſcript ſome years ago, and to which I have ſince made very large additions.

G

I.

Ariſe, my tend'reſt thoughts, ariſe,
To torrents, melt my ſtreaming eyes!
And thou, my heart, with anguiſh feel
Thoſe evils which thou canſt not heal!

II.

See human nature ſunk in ſhame!
See ſcandals pour'd on Jeſus' name!
The Father wounded through the Son!
The world abus'd, the ſoul undone!

III.

See the ſhort courſe of vain delight
Cloſing in everlaſting night!
In flames, that no abatement know,
The briny tears for ever flow.

IV.

My God, I feel the mournful ſcene;
My bowels yearn o'er dying men:
And fain my pity would reclaim,
And ſnatch the fire-brands from the flame.

V.

But feeble my compaſſion proves,
And can but weep, where moſt it loves.
Thine own all ſaving arm employ,
And turn theſe drops of grief to joy!

§. 102. The Colonel, immediately after the concluſion of the ſervice, met me in the veſtry, and embraced me in the moſt obliging and affectionate manner, as if there had been a long friendſhip between us; aſſured me, that he had for ſome years been intimately acquainted with my writings; and deſired, that we might concert meaſures for ſpending ſome hours together before I left the town. I was ſo happy, as to be able to ſecure an opportunity of doing it; and I muſt leave it upon record, that I cannot recollect, I was ever equally edified by any converſation I remember to have enjoyed. We paſſed that evening and the next morning together; and it is impoſſible for me to deſcribe the impreſſion, which the interview left upon my heart. I rode alone all the remainder of the day; and it was my unſpeakable happineſs that I was alone, ſince I could be no longer with him: for I can hardly conceive, what other company would not then have been an incumbrance. The views which he gave me even then, (for he began to repose a moft obliging confidence in me, though he concealed fome of the moft extraordinary circumftances of the methods by which he had been recovered to God and happinefs) with thefe cordial fentiments of evangelical piety and extenfive goodnefs, which he poured out into my bofom with fo endearing a freedom, fired my very foul ; and I hope I may truly fay, (what I with and pray, many of my readers may alfo adopt for themfelves,) that I glorified God in him. Our epiftolary correfpondence immediately commenced upon my return ; and though, through the multiplicity of bufinefs on both fides, it fuffered many interruptions ; it was in fome degree the blefling of all the following years of my life, till he fell by thofe unreafonable and wicked men, who had it in their hearts with him to have deftroyed all our glory, defence, and happinefs.

§. 103. The firft letter I received from him was fo remarkable, that fome perfons of eminent piety, to whom I communicated it, would not be content without copying it out, or making fome extracts from it. I perfuade myfelf, that my devout reader will not be difpleafed, that I infert the greateft part of it here ; efpecially, as it ferves to illuftrate the affectionate fenfe which he had of the divine goodnefs in his converfion, though more than twenty years had paffed fince that memorable event happened. Having mentioned my ever dear and honoured friend, Dr, Ifaac Watts, on an occafion which I hinted above, (§. 70) he adds, " I have " been in pain for feveral years, left that excellent perfon, " that fweet finger in our Ifrael, fhould have been called to " heaven, before I had an opportunity of letting him know, " how much his works have been bleffed to me, and of courfe, " of returning him my hearty thanks : For though it is ow- " ing to the operation of the blefled Spirit, that any thing " works effectually upon our hearts, yet if we are not thankful " to the inftrument which God is pleafed to make ufe of, when " we do fee, how fhall we be thankful to the Almighty, " whom we have not feen ? I defire to blefs God for the " good news of his recovery, and intreat you to tell him, " that although I cannot keep pace with him here, in ce- " lebrating the high praifes of our glorious Redeemer, which " is the greateft grief of my heart ; yet I am perfuaded, that

" when I join the glorious company above, where there
" will be no draw-backs, none will out-sing me there ; be-
" cause I shall not find any that will be more indebted to
" the wonderful riches of divine grace than I.

> " Give me a place at thy saints feet,
> " Or some fail'n angel's vacant seat ;
> " I'll strive to sing as loud as they,
> " Who sit above in brighter day.

" I know, it is natural for every one, who has felt the Al-
" mighty power which raised our glorious Redeemer from
" the grave, to believe his case singular : But I have made
" every one in this respect submit, as soon as he has heard
" my story.   And if you seemed so surprized at the account
" which I gave you, what will you be when you hear it all ?

> " Oh if I had an angel's voice,
> " And could be heard from pole to pole ;
> " I would to all the listening world
> " Proclaim thy goodness to my soul."

He then concludes. (after some expressions of endearment,
which, with whatever pleasure I review them, I must not
here insert ;) " If you knew what a natural aversion I have
" to writing, you would be astonished at the length of this
" letter, which is I believe the longest I ever wrote.   But
" my heart warms when I write to you, which makes my
" pen move the easier.   I hope, it will please our gracious
" God, long to preserve you, a blessed instrument in his
" hand of doing great good in the church of Christ ; and
" that you may always enjoy a thriving soul in a healthful
" body, shall be the continual prayer of, &c."

§. 104. As our intimacy grew, our mutual affection in-
creased ; and " my dearest friend" was the form of address,
with which most of his epistles of the last years were begun,
and ended.   Many of them are filled up with his sentiments
of those writings which I published during these years, which
he read with great attention, and of which he speaks in
terms, which it becomes me to suppress, and to impute it
in a considerable degree to the kind prejudices of so endeared a friendship.   He gives me repeated assurances,

" that he was daily mindful of me in his prayers ;" a circumſtance, which I cannot recollect without the greateſt
thankfulneſs ; the loſs of which I ſhould more deeply lament,
did I not hope, that the happy effect of theſe prayers might
ſtill continue, and might run into all my remaining days.

§. 105. It might be a pleaſure to me, to make ſeveral
extracts from many others of his letters : But it is a pleaſure which I ought to ſuppreſs, and rather to reflect with
unfeigned humility, how unworthy I was of ſuch regards
from ſuch a perſon, and of that divine goodneſs which gave me
ſuch a friend in him. I ſhall therefore only add two general
remarks, which offer themſelves from ſeveral of his letters.
The one is, that there is in ſome of them, as our freedom increaſed an agreeable vein of humour and pleaſantry ; which
ſhews, how eaſy religion ſat upon him, and how far he
was from placing any part of it in a gloomy melancholy, or
ſtiff formality. The other is, that he frequently refers to
domeſtic circumſtances ſuch as the illneſs or recovery of my
children, &c. which I am ſurprized how a man of his extenſive and important buſineſs could ſo diſtinctly bear upon
his mind. But his memory was good, and his heart was
yet better ; and his friendſhip was ſuch, that nothing which
ſenſibly affected the heart of one whom he honoured with it,
left his own but ſlightly touched. I have all imaginable reaſon to believe, that in many inſtances his prayers were not
only offered for us in general terms, but varied as our particular ſituation required. Many quotations might verify
this ; but I decline troubling the reader with an enumeration
of paſſages, in which it was only the abundance of friendly
ſympathy, that gave this truly great, as well as good man,
ſo cordial a concern.

§. 106. After this correſpondence, carried on for the
ſpace of about three years, and ſome interviews which we
had enjoyed at different places, he came to ſpend ſome time
with us at Northampton, and brought with him his lady, and
his two eldeſt children. I had here an opportunity of taking a
much nearer view of his character, and ſurveying it in a
much greater variety of lights than before ; and my eſteem
for him increaſed, in proportion to theſe opportunities.
What I have wrote above, with reſpect to his conduct in relative life, was in a great meaſure drawn from what I now

ſaw. And I ſhall here mention ſome other points in his behaviour, which particularly ſtruck my mind; and likewiſe
ſhall touch on his ſentiments on ſome topics of importance,
which he freely communicated to me, and which I remarked
on account of that wiſdom and propriety, which I apprehended in them.

§. 107. There was nothing more openly obſervable in
Colonel Gardiner, than the exemplary gravity, compoſure,
and reverence, with which he attended public worſhip Copious as he was in his ſecret devotions before he engaged in
it, he always began them ſo early, as not to be retarded by
them, when he ſhould reſort to the houſe of God. He, and
all his ſoldiers who choſe to worſhip with him, were generally there, (as I have already hinted,) before the ſervice
begin; that the entrance of ſo many of them at once might
not diſturb the congregation already engaged in devotion, and
that there might be the better opportunity for bringing the
mind to a becoming attention, and preparing it for converſe
with the divine Being. While acts of worſhip were going
on, whether of prayer or ſinging, he always ſtood up; and
whatever regard he might have for perſons who paſſed by
him at that time, though it were to come into the ſame pew,
he never paid any compliment to them: And often has he
expreſſed his wonder at the indecorum, of breaking off our
addreſs to God, to bow to a fellow creature; which he
thought a much greater indecency, than it would be, on a like
occaſion and circumſtance, to interrupt an addreſs to our
prince. During the time of preaching, his eye was commonly fixed upon the miniſter, though ſometimes turned
round upon the auditory. where if he obſerved any to trifle,
it filled him with juſt indignation. And I have known inſtances, in which upon making the remark, he has communicated it to ſome friend of the perſons who were guilty of it,
that proper application might be made to prevent it for the
time to come.

§. 108. A more devout communicant at the table of the
Lord has perhaps ſeldom been any where known. Often
have I had the pleaſure, to ſee that manly countenance ſoft-
ened to all the marks of humiliation and contrition, on this
occaſion; and to diſcern, in ſpite of all his efforts to conceal them, ſtreams of tears flowing down from his eyes,
while he has been directing them to thoſe memorials of his

Redeemer's love And fome, who have conve:fed intimately with him after he came from that ordinance, have obferved a vifible abftraction from furrounding obj-cts ; by which there feemed reafon to imagine, that his foul was wrapped up in holy contemplation And I particularly remember, that when we had once fpent great part of the following Monday in riding together, he made an apology to me for being fo abfent as he feemed, by telling me, " that his heart was " flown upwards before he was aware, to him whom not " having feen he loved ;[*] and that he was rejoicing in him " with fuch unfpeakable joy, that he could not hold it down " to creature converfe."

§. 109. In all the offices of friendfhip he was remarkably ready, and had a moft fweet and engaging manner of performing them, which greatly heightened the obligations he conferred. He feemed not to fet any high value upon any benefit he beftowed ; but did it without the leaft parade, as a thing which in thofe circumftances came of courfe, where he had profeffed love and refpect ; which he was not over-forward to do, though he treated ftrangers, and thofe who were moft his inferiors, very courteoufly and always feemed, becaufe he in truth always was, glad of any opportunity of doing them good.

§. 110 He was particularly zealous in vindicating the reputation of his friends in their abfence : And though I cannot recollect, that I had ever an opportunity of obferving this immediately, as I don't know that I ever was prefent with him when any ill was fpoken of others at all ; yet by what I have heard him fay, with relation to attempts to injure the character of worthy and ufeful men, I have reafon to believe, that no man living was more fenfible of the bafenefs and infamy, as well as the cruelty, of fuch a conduct. He knew, and defpifed, the low principles of refentment for unreafonable expectations difappointed, of perfonal attachment to men of fome crffing interefts, of envy, and of party zeal, from whence fuch a conduct often proceeds ; and was particularly offended, when he found it (as he frequently did,) in perfons that fet up for the greateft patrons of liberty, virtue, and candor. He looked upon the mur-

* N. B. This alluded to the fubject of the fermon the day before, which was 1 Pet. i. 8.

therers of reputation and uſefulneſs, as ſome of the vileſt
peſts of ſociety; and plainly ſhewed on every proper occaſion, that he thought it the part of a generous, benevolent,
and couragious man, to exert himſelf in tracing and hunt-
ing down the ſlander, that the authors or abetters of it might
be leſs capable of doing miſchief for the future.

§. 111. The moſt plauſible objection that I ever heard to
Colonel Gardiner's character is, that he was too much attached to ſome religious principles, eſtabliſhed indeed in the
churches, both of England and Scotland, but which have
of late years been much diſputed, and from which, it is at
leaſt generally ſuppoſed not a few in both have thought proper to depart; whatever expedients they may have found
to quiet their conſciences, in ſubſcribing thoſe formularies,
in which they are plainly taught. His zeal was eſpecially
apparent in oppoſition to thoſe doctrines, which ſeemed to
derogate from the divine honours of the Son and Spirit of
God, and from the freedom of divine grace, or the reality
and neceſſity of its operations, in the converſion and ſalvation of ſinners.

§ 112. With relation to theſe I muſt obſerve, that it
was his moſt ſtedfaſt perſuaſion, that all thoſe notions,
which repreſent our bleſſed Redeemer and the holy Spirit
as mere creatures, or which ſet aſide the atonement of the
former, or the influences of the latter, do ſap the very
foundation of chriſtianity by rejecting the moſt glorious
doctrines peculiar to it. He had attentively obſerved (what
indeed is too obvious.) the unhappy influence, which the
denial of theſe principles often has on the character of miniſters, and on their ſucceſs; and was perſuaded, that an
attempt to ſubſtitute that mutilated form of chriſtianity
which remains, when theſe eſſentials of it are taken away,
has proved one of the moſt ſucceſsful methods which the
great enemy of ſouls has ever taken in theſe latter days, to
lead men by inſenſible degrees into deiſm, vice, and perdi-
tion. He alſo ſagaciouſly obſerved the artful manner in
which obnoxious tenets are often maintained or inſinuated,
with all that mixture of zeal and addreſs with which they
are propagated in the world, even by thoſe who had moſt
ſolemnly profeſſed to believe, and engaged to teach the contrary : And as he really apprehended, that the glory of
God, and the ſalvation of ſouls was concerned, his piety

and charity made him eager and ſtrenuous in oppoſing, what
he judged to be errors of ſo pernicious a nature.   Yet I muſt
declare, that according to what I have known of him, (and
I believe he opened his heart on theſe topics to me, with
as much freedom as to any man living,) he was not ready
upon light ſuſpicions to charge tenets which he thought ſo
pernicious on any, eſpecially where he ſaw the appearances
of a good temper and life, which he always reverenced and
loved in perſons of all ſentiments and profeſſions.   He ſe-
verely condemned cauſeleſs jealouſies, and evil ſurmiſings
of every kind ; and extended that charity in this reſpect,
both to clergy, and laity, which good biſhop Burnet was ſo
ready, according to his own account. to limit to the latter,
" of believing every man good till he knew him to be bad,
" and his notions right till he knew them wrong."   He
could not but be very ſenſible of the unhappy conſequences,
which may follow on attacking the characters of men, eſpecially of thoſe who are miniſters of the goſpel : And if
through a mixture of human frailty, from which the beſt of
men in the beſt of their meanings and intentions are not
entirely free, he has ever. in the warmth of his heart,
dropped a word which might be injurious to any other on
that account, (which I believe very ſeldom happened.) he
would gladly retract it on better information ; which was
perfectly agreeable to that honeſt and generous frankneſs
of temper, in which I never knew any man who exceeded
him.

§. 113. On the whole, it was indeed his deliberate judgment, that the Arian, Socinian, and Pelagian doctrines were
highly diſhonourable to God, and dangerous to the ſouls of
men ; and that it was the duty of private chriſtians, to be
greatly on their guard againſt thoſe miniſters by whom they
are entertained, leſt their minds ſhould be corrupted from
the ſimplicity that is in Chriſt.   Yet he ſincerely abhorred
the thought of perſecution for conſcience ſake ; of the abſurdity and iniquity of which in all its kinds and degrees,
he had as deep and rational a conviction, as any man I
could name.   And indeed the generoſity of his heroic heart
could hardly bear to think, that thoſe glorious truths. which
he ſo cordially loved and which he aſſuredly believed to be
capable of ſuch fair ſupport, both from reaſon and the word
of God, ſhould be diſgraced by methods of defence and

propagation, common to the moſt impious and ridiculous falſehoods. Nor did he by any means approve of paſſionate and furious ways of vindicating the moſt vital and important doctrines of the goſpel : For he knew, that to maintain the moſt benevolent religion in the world, by ſuch malevolent and internal methods, was deſtroying the end to accompliſh the means; and that it was as impoſſible, that true chriſtianity ſhould be ſupported thus, as it is that a man ſhould long be nouriſhed by eating his own fleſh. To diſplay the genuine fruits of chriſtianity in a good life, to be ready to plead with meekneſs and ſweetneſs for the doctrines it teaches, and to labour by every office of humanity and goodneſs to gain upon them that oppoſe it, were the weapons with which this good ſoldier of Jeſus Chriſt faithfully fought the battles of the Lord. Theſe weapons will always be victorious in his cauſe; and they who have recourſe to others of a different temperature, how ſtrong ſoever they may ſeem, and how ſharp ſoever they may really be, will find they break in their hands when they exert them moſt furiouſly, and are much more likely to wound themſelves, than to conquer the enemies they oppoſe.

§. 114. But while I am ſpeaking of Colonel Gardiner's charity in this reſpect, I muſt not omit that of another kind, which has indeed engroſſed the name of charity much more than it ought, excellent as it is ; I mean alms-giving, for which he was very remarkable. I have ofen wondered, how he was able to do ſo many generous things this way : But his frugality fed the ſpring. He made no pleaſurable expence on himſelf, and was contented with a very decent appearance in his family, without effecting ſuch an air of grandeur, as could not have been ſupported without ſacrificing to it ſatisfactions far nobler, and to a temper like his far more delightful. The lively and tender feelings of his heart in favour of the diſtreſſed and afflicted, made it a ſelf indulgence to him to relieve them ; and the deep conviction he had of the vain and tranſitory nature of the enjoyments of this world, together with the ſublime view he had of another, engaged him to diſpenſe his bounties with a very liberal hand, and even to ſeek out proper objects of them : And above all, his ſincere and ardent love to the Lord Jeſus Chriſt engaged him to feel, with a true ſympathy, the concerns of his poor members. In conſequence of this, he honoured feveral of his friends with commiffions for the relief of the poor ; and particularly, with relation to fome under my paftoral care, he referred it to my difcretion to fupply them with what I fhould judge expedient, and frequently preffed me in his letters to be fure not to let them want. And where perfons ftanding in need of his charity happened, as they often did, to be perfons of remarkably religious difpofitions, it was eafy to perceive, that he not only loved, but honoured them; and really efteemed it an honour which providence conferred upon him, that he fhould be made, as it were, the almoner of God for the relief of fuch.

§. 115. I cannot forbear relating a little ftory here, which, when the Colonel himfelf heard it, gave him fuch exquifite pleafure, that I hope it will be acceptable to feveral of my readers. There was in a village, about three miles from Northampton, and in a family which of all others near me was afterwards moft indebted to him, (though he had never then feen any member of it,) an aged and poor, but eminently good woman, who had with great difficulty, in the exercife of much faith and patience, diligence and humility, made fhift to educate a large family of children, after the death of her hufband, without being chargeable to the parifh; which, as it was quite beyond her hope, fhe often fpoke of with great delight At length, when worn out with age and infirmities, fhe lay upon her dying bed, fhe did in a moft lively and affecting manner exprefs her hope and joy in the views of approaching glory. Yet amidft all the triumph of fuch a profpect, there was one remaining care and diftrefs which lay heavy on her mind ; which was, that her journey and her ftock of provifions were both ended together ; fhe feared, that fhe muft either be buried at the parifh expence, or leave her moft dutiful and affectionate daughters the houfe ftripped of fome of the few moveables which remained in it, to perform the laft office of duty to her, which fhe had reafon to believe they would do. While fhe was combating with this only remaining anxiety I happened, though I knew not the extremity of her illnefs, to come in, and to bring with me a guinea, which the generous Colonel had fent by a fpecial meffage, on hearing the character of the family, for its relief. A prefent like this, (probably the moft confiderable they had ever received in their lives,)

coming in this manner from an entire stranger, at such a
crefis of time, threw my dying friend, (for such, amidst
all her poverty, I rejoiced to call her,) into a perfect tranfport of joy. She esteemed it a fingular favor of Providence,
fent to her in her laft moments as a token for good, and
greeted it as a fpecial mark of that loving-kindnefs of God
which fhould attend her for ever. She would therefore be
raifed up in her bed, that fhe might blefs God for it upon
her knees, a d with her laft breath pray for her kind and
generous benefactor, and for him who had been the inftrument of directing his bounty into this channel. After which
fhe foon expired, with fuch tranquility and fweetnefs, as
could not but moft fenfibly delight all who beheld her, and
occafioned many, who knew the circumftances, to glorify
God on her behalf,

§. 116. The Colonel's laft refidence at Northampton was
in June and July, 1742, when Lord Cadogan's regiment
of dragoons was quartered here: And I cannot but obferve
that wherever that regiment came, it was remarkable, not
only for the fine appearance it made, and for the exactnefs
with which it performed its various exercifes, (of which it
had about this time the honor to receive the moft illuftrious
teftimonials;) but alfo for the great fobriety and regularity
of the foldiers. Many of the officers copied after the excellent pattern, which they had daily before their eyes; and
a confiderable number of the private men feemed to be perfons, not only of ftrict virtue, but of ferious piety. And I
doubt not, but they found their abundant account in it; not
only in the ferenity and happinefs of their own minds, which
is beyond comparifon the moft important confideration; but
alfo in fome degree, in the obliging and refpectful treatment
which they generally met with in their quarters. And I
mention this, becaufe I am perfuaded, that if gentlemen of
their profeffion knew, and would reflect, how much more
comfortable they make their own quarters by a fober, orderly, and obliging conduct, they would be regular out of mere
felf-love; if they were not influenced, as I heartily wifh
they may always be, by a nobler principle.

§. 117. Towards the latter end of this year he embark-
ed for Flanders, and fpent fome confierable time with the
regiment at Ghent; where he much regretted the want of
thofe religious ordinances and opportunities, which had made

his other abodes delightful. But as he had made fo eminent a progrefs in that divine life, which they are all intended to promote, he could not be unactive in the caufe of God. I have now before me a letter dated from thence, October 16, 1742, in which he writes: " As for me, I am indeed " in a dry and barren land, where no water is, Rivers of " waters run down mine eyes, becaufe nothing is to be " heard in our Sodom, but blafpheming the name of my " God; and I am not honoured as the inftrument of doing " any great fervice. 'Tis true I have reformed fix or feven " field-officers of fwearing. I dine every day with them, " and have entered them into a voluntary contract, to pay " a fhilling to the poor for every oath ; and it is wonderful " to obferve the effect it has had already. One of them told " me this day at dinner, that it had really fuch an influence " upon him, that being at cards laft night when another of- " ficer fell a fwearing, he was not able to bear it, but rofe " up and left the company. So you fee, reftraints at firft a- " rifing from a low principle may improve into fomething " better."

§. 118. During his abode here, he had a great deal of bufinefs upon his hands ; and had alfo, in fome marches, the care of more regiments than his own: And it has been very delightful to me to obferve, what a degree of converfe with heaven, and the God of it, he maintained, amidft thefe fcenes of hurry and fatigue ; of which the reader may find a remarkable fpecimen in the following letter, dated from Lichwick, in the beginning of April, 1743, which was one of the laft I received from him while abroad, and begins with thefe words. " Yefterday being the Lord's day, at fix in " the morning, I had the pleafure of receiving yours at Nor- " tonick ; and it proved a Sabbath-day's blefling to me. " Some time before it reached me," (from whence by the way it may be obferved, that his former cuftom of rifing fo early to his devotions was ftill retained,) " I had been " wreftling with God with many tears ; when I had read " it, I returned to my knees again, to give hearty thanks " to him, for all his goodnefs to you and yours, and alfo to " myfelf, in that he hath been pleafed to ftir up fo many " who are dear to him, to be mindful of me at the throne " of grace." And then, after the mention of fome other

H

particulars, he adds; " Bleſſed, and adored for ever, be the
" holy name of my heavenly Father, who holds my ſoul in
" life, and my body in perfect health ! Were I to recount
" his mercy and goodneſs to me even in the midſt of all
" theſe hurries, I ſhould never have done.—I hope, your
" matter will ſtill encourage you in his work, and make
" you a bleſſing to many. My deareſt friend, I am much,
" more yours than I can expreſs, and ſhall remain ſo while
" I am, J. G."

§. 119. In this correſpondence I had a farther opportunity
of diſcovering that humble reſignation to the will of God,
which made ſo amiable a part of his character, and of which
I had before ſeen ſo many inſtances.   He ſpeaks in the letter from which I have juſt been giving an extract, of the
hope he had expreſſed in a former, of ſeeing us again that
winter ; and he adds, " To be ſure, it would have been a
" great pleaſure to me : But we poor mortals form projects,
" and the Almighty ruler of the univerſe diſpoſes of all as
" he pleaſes.   A great many of us were getting ready for
" our return to England, when we received an order to
" march towards Frankfort, to the great ſurprize of the
" whole army, neither can any of us comprehend what we
" are to do there ; for there is no enemy in that country,
" the French army being marched into Batavia, where I am
" ſure we cannot follow them.   But it is the will of the
" Lord ; and his will be done ! I deſire to bleſs and praiſe
" my heavenly Father, that I am entirely reſigned to it.
" It is no matter where I go, or what becomes of me, ſo
" that God may be glorified, in my life, or my death.   I
" ſhould rejoice much to hear, that all my friends were e-
" qually reſigned."

§. 120. The mention of this article reminds me of another, relating to the views which he had of obtaining a regiment for himſelf.   He endeavoured to deſerve it by the moſt
faithful ſervices ; ſome of them indeed beyond what the
ſtrength of his conſtitution could well bear : for the weather
in ſome of theſe marches proved exceeding bad, and yet he
would be always at the head of his people, that he might
look to every thing that concerned them, with the exacteſt
care.   This obliged him to neglect the beginnings of a fe-
veriſh illneſs ; the natural conſequence of which was, that it

grew very formidable, forced a long confinement upon him, and gave animal nature a shock, which it never recovered.

§. 121. In the mean time, as he had the promise of a regiment before he quitted England, his friends were continually expecting an occasion of congratulating him on having received the command of one. But still they were disappointed; and on some of them the disappointment seemed to sit heavy. As for the Colonel himself, he seemed quite easy about it; and appeared much greater in that easy situation of mind, than the highest military honours and preferments could have made him. With great pleasure do I at this moment recollect the unaffected serenity, and even indifference, with which he expresses himself on this occasion, in a letter to me, dated about the beginning of April, 1743; "The "disappointment of a regiment is nothing to me; for I am "satisfied, that had it been for God's glory, I should have "had it; and I should have been sorry to have had it on "any other terms. My heavenly Father has bestowed up- "on me infinitely more, than if he had made me emperor "of the whole world."

§. 122. I find several parallel expressions in other letters; and those to his lady about the same time were just in the same strain. In an extract from one, which was written from Aix la-Chapelle, April 21, the same year, I meet with these words: "People here imagine I must be sadly "troubled, that I have not got a regiment, (for six out of "seven vacant are now disposed of,) but they are strangely "mistaken, for it has given me no sort of trouble. My hea- "venly Father knows what is best for me; and blessed and "for ever adored be his name, he has given me an entire "resignation to his will: besides I don't know, that ever I "met with any disappointment since I was a Christian, but "it pleased God to discover to me, that it was plainly for "my advantage, by bestowing something better upon me "afterwards: many instances of which I am able to pro- "duce; and therefore I should be the greatest of monsters, "if I did not trust in him."

§. 123. I should be guilty of a great omission, if I were not to add, how remarkably the event corresponded with his faith, on this occasion. For whereas he had no intimation or expectation, of any thing more than a regiment of foot, his majesty was pleased, out of his great goodness, to give him a regiment of dragoons, which was then quartered just in his own neighbourhood. And it is properly remarked by the reverend and worthy person through whose hand this letter was transmitted to me, that when the Colonel thus expressed himself, he could have no prospect of what he afterwards so soon obtained; as General Bland's regiment, to which he was advanced, was only vacant on the 19th of April, that is, two days before the date of this letter, when it was impossible he should have any notice of that vacancy. And it also deserves observation, that some few days after the Colonel was thus unexpectedly promoted to the command of these dragoons, Brigadier Cornwallis's regiment of foot, then in Flanders, became vacant: now had this happened before his promotion to General Bland's, Colonel Gardiner in all probability would only have had that regiment of foot, and so have continued in Flanders. When the affair was issued, he informs lady Frances of it, in a letter dated from a village near Frankfort, May 3, in which he refers to his former of the 21st of April, observing how remarkably it was verified, " in God's having given him," (for so he expresses it, agreeably to the views he continually maintained of the universal agency of divine Providence,) " what he " had no expectation of, and what was so much better than " that which he had missed, a regiment of dragoons quar- " tered at his own door."

§. 124. It appeared to him, that by this remarkable event Providence called him home. Accordingly, though he had other preferments offered him in the army, he chose to return; and I believe, the more willingly, as he did not expect there would have been any action. Just at this time it pleased God to give him an awful instance of the uncertainty of human prospects and enjoyments, by that violent fever, which seized him at Ghent in his way to England; and perhaps the more severely, for the efforts he made to push on his journey, though he had for some days been much indisposed. It was, I think, one of the first fits of severe illness he had ever met with; and he was ready to look upon it, as a sudden call into eternity: But it gave him no painful alarm in that view. He committed himself to the God of his life, and in a few weeks he was so well recovered, as to be capable of pursuing his journey, though not without difficulty: And I cannot but think, it might have conduced much to a more perfect recovery than he ever attained, to have allowed himfelf a longer repofe, in order to recruit his exhaufted ftrength and fpirits. But there was an activity in his temper, not eafy to be reftrained; and it was now fti-mulated, not only by a defire of feeing his friends, but of being with his regiment; that he might omit nothing in his power, to regulate their morals and their difcipline, and to form them for public fervice. Accordingly he paffed through London, about the middle of June, 1743, where he had the honor of waiting on their royal highneffes the Prince and Princefs of Wales, and of receiving from both the moft o-bliging tokens of favor and efteem. He arrived at North-ampton on Monday the 20th of June, and fpent part of three days here. But the great pleafure which his return and preferment gave us, was much abated, by obferving his countenance fo fadly altered, and many marks of languor, and remaining diforder, which evidently appeared; fo that he really looked ten years older than he had done ten months before. I had however a fatisfaction, fufficient to counter-balance much of the concern which this alteration gave me, in a renewed opportunity of obferving, indeed more fenfibly than ever, in how remarkable a degree he was dead to the enjoyments and views of this mortal life. When I congra-tulated him on the favorable appearances of Providence for him in the late event, he briefly told me the remarkable circumftances that attended it, with the moft genuine im-preffions of gratitude to God for them; but added, " that " as his account was increafed with his income, power, and " influence, and his cares were proportionably increafed too, " it was as to his own perfonal concern much the fame to " him, whether he had remained in his former ftation, or " been elevated to this; but that if God fhould by this " means honor him, as an inftrument of doing more good " than he could otherwife have done, he fhould rejoice in " it."

§. 125. I perceived that the near views he had taken of eternity, in the illnefs from which he was then fo imperfectly recovered had not in the leaft alarmed him; but that he would have been entirely willing, had fuch been the deter-mination of God, to have been cut fhort in a foreign land, without any earthly friend near him, and in the midft of a journey, undertaken with hopes and prospects so pleasing to nature; which appeared to me no inconsiderable evidence of the strength of his faith. But we shall wonder the less at this extraordinary resignation, if we consider the joyful and assured prospect which he had of an happiness infinitely superior beyond the grave; of which that worthy minister of the church of Scotland, who had an opportunity of conversing with him quickly after his return, and having the memorable story of his conversion from his own mouth, (as I have hinted above,) writes thus in his letter to me, dated Jan. 14, 1746 7 ' When he came to review his regiment " in Linlithgow, in summer 1743 after having given me " the wonderful story as above, he concluded in words to "" this purpose;—Let me die whenever it shall please God. or " wherever it shall be, I am sure, I shall go to the man- " sions of eternal glory, and enjoy my God and my Redeem- " er in heaven for ever "

§. 126. While he was with us at this time, he appeared deeply affected with the sad state of things as to religion and morals; and seemed to apprehend, that the rod of God was hanging over so sinful a nation. He observed a great deal of disaffection, which the enemies of the government had, by a variety of artifices, been raising in Scotland for some years; and the number of Jacobites there, together with the defenceless state in which our island then was, with respect to the number of its forces at home, (of which he spoke at once with great concern and astonishment,) led him to expect an invasion from France, and an attempt in favor of the pretender, much sooner than it happened. I have heard him say, many years before it came so near being accomplished, " that a few thousands might have a fair chance for " marching from Edinburgh to London uncontrolled, and " throw the whole kingdom into an astonishment " And I have great reason to believe, that this was one main consideration, which engaged him to make such haste to his regiment, then quartered in those parts; as he imagined there was not a spot of ground, where he might be more like to have a call to expose his life in the service of his country; and perhaps, by appearing on a proper call early in its defence, be instrumental in suppressing the beginnings of most formidable mischiefs. How rightly he judged in these things, the event did too evidently show.

§. 127. The evening before our laſt ſeparation, as I knew I could not entertain the invaluable friend who was then my gueſt more agreeably, I preached a ſermon in my own houſe, with ſome peculiar reference to his caſe and circumſtances, from thoſe ever memorable words than which I have never felt any more powerful and more comfortable: Pſal. xci. 14, 15, 16. "Becauſe he hath ſet his love upon me, therefore will I deliver him ; I will ſet him on high, becauſe he hath known my name : He ſhall call upon me, and I will anſwer him : I will be with him in trouble, I will deliver him, and honour him : With long life (or length of days) will I ſatisfy him, and ſhew him my ſalvation." This ſcripture could not but lead our meditations to ſurvey the character of the good man, as one who ſo knows the name of the bleſſed God, (has ſuch a deep apprehenſion of the glories and perfections of his nature,) as determinately to ſet his love upon him. to make him the ſupreme object of his moſt ardent and conſtant affection. And it ſuggeſted the moſt ſublime and animating hopes to perſons of ſuch a character ; that their prayers ſhall be always acceptable to God ; that though they may, and muſt be called out to their ſhare in the troubles and calamities of life, yet they may aſſure themſelves of the divine preſence in all ; which ſhall iſſue in their deliverance, in their exaltation, ſometimes. to diſtinguiſhed honour and eſteem among men. and, it may be, in a long courſe of uſeful and happy years on earth ; at leaſt, which ſhall undoubtedly end in ſeeing, to their perpetual delight, the complete ſalvation of God, in a world where they ſhall enjoy length of days for ever and ever, and employ them all in adoring the great author of their ſaivation and felicity. It is evident, that theſe natural thoughts on ſuch a ſcripture were matters of univerſal concern. Yet had I known, that this was the laſt time I ſhould ever addreſs Colonel Gardiner. as a miniſter of the goſpel, and had I foreſeen the ſcenes through which God was about to lead him, I hardly know what conſiderations I could have ſuggeſted with more peculiar propriety. The attention, elevation, and delight, with which he heard them, was very apparent; and the pleaſure which the obſervation of it gave me, continues to this moment. And let me be permitted to digreſs ſo far, as to add, that this is indeed the great ſupport of a chriſtian miniſter, under the many diſcouragements and diſappointments which he meets with, in his attempts to fix upon the proiligate or the thoughtlefs part of mankind a deep fenfe of religious truths ; that there is another important part of his work, in which he may hope to be more generallly fuc-cefsful ; as by plain, artlefs, but ferious difcourfes, the great principles of chriftian duty and hope may be nourifhed and invigorated in good men, their graces watered as at the root, and their fouls animated, both to perfevere, and improve in holinefs. And when we are effectually per-forming fuch benevolent offices, fo well fuiting our immor-tal natures, to perfons whofe hearts are cementcd with ours in the bonds of the moft endearing and facred friendihip, it is too little to fay, it over-pays the fatigue of our labours ; it even fwallows up all fenfe of it, in the moft rational and fublime pleafure

§. 128. An incident occurs to my mind, which happen-ed that evening, which at leaft for the oddnefs of it may deferve a place in thefe memoirs.   I had then with me one Thomas Porter, a poor, but very honeft and religious man, (now living at Hatfield-Broadoak in Effex,) who is quite unacquainted with letters, fo as not to be able to diftinguifh one from another ; yet is mafter of the contents of the bible in fo extraordinary a degree, that he has not only fixed an immenfe number of texts in his memory, but merely by hearing them quoted in fermons has regiftered there the chapter and verfe, in which thefe paffages are to be found : This is attended with a marvellous facility in directing thofe that can read, to turn to them, and a moft unaccountable talent of fixing on fuch, as fuit almoft every imaginable variety of circumftances in common life   There are two confiderations in his cafe, which make it the more wonder-ful : The one, that he is a perfon of a very low genius, having, befides a ftammering which makes his fpeech al-moft unintelligible to ftrangers, fo wild and aukward a manner of behaviour, that he is frequently taken for an idiot, and feems in many things to be indeed fo : The other, that he grew up to manhood in a very licentious courfe of living, and an entire ignorance of divine things, fo that all thefe exact impreffions on his memory have been made in his riper years.   I thought it would not be difagreeable to the Colonel, to introduce to him this odd phænomenon, which many hundreds of people have had a curiofity to ex-

amine : And among all the ſtrange things I have ſeen in
him, I never remember any which equalled what paſſed on
this occaſion. On hearing the colonel's profeſſion, and receiving ſome hints of his religious character, he ran through
a vaſt variety of ſcriptures, beginning at the Pentateuch
and going on to the Revelation, relating either to the dependance to be fixed on God for the ſucceſs of military preparations, or to the inſtances and promiſes occurring there
of his care of good men in the moſt eminent dangers, or to
the encouragement to deſpiſe perils and death, while engaged
in a good cauſe, and ſupported by the views of a happy immortality. I believe, he quoted more than twenty of theſe
paſſages; and I muſt freely own, that I know not who could
have choſe them with greater propriety. If my memory do
not deceive me, the laſt of this catalogue was that from
which I afterwards preached on the lamented occaſion of
this great man's fall : Be thou faithful unto death, and I will
give thee a crown of life. We were all aſtoniſhed at ſo remarkable a fact ; and I queſtion not, but that many of my
readers will think the memory of it worthy of being thus
preſerved.

§ 129. But to return to my main ſubject : The next
day after the ſermon and converſation of which I have been
ſpeaking, I took my laſt leave of my ineſtimable friend, after attending him ſome part of his way northward. The
firſt ſtage of our journey was to the cottage of that poor, but
very religious family, which I had acceſion to mention above,
as relieved, and indeed in a great meaſure ſubſiſted, by his
charity. And nothing could be more delightful, than to obſerve the condeſcenſion, with which he converſed with theſe
his humble penſioners. We there put up our laſt united prayers together, and he afterwards expreſſed, in the ſtrongeſt
terms I ever heard him uſe on ſuch an occaſion, the ſingular
pleaſure with which he had joined in them. Indeed it was no
ſmall ſatisfaction to me, to have an opportunity of recommending ſuch a valuable friend to the divine protection and bleſſing,
with that particular freedom, and enlargement on what was
peculiar in his circumſtances, which hardly any other ſituation, unleſs we had been quite alone, could ſo conveniently
have admitted We went from thence to the table of a perſon of diſtinction in the neighbourhood : where he had an
opportunity of ſhewing, in how decent and graceful a man-

ner he could unite the Chriftian and the gentleman, and give
converfation an improved and religious turn, without violat-
ing any of the rules of polite behaviour, or faying or doing
any thing which looked at all conftrained or affected. Here
we took our laft embrace, committing each other to the care
of the God of heaven; and the Colonel purfued his journey
to the north, where he fpent all the remainder of his days.

§. 130. The more I reflect upon this appointment of providence, the more I difcern of the beauty and wifdom of it;
not only as it led directly to that glorious period of life, with
which God had determined to honour him, and in which, I
think, it becomes all his friends to rejoice; but alfo, as the
retirement on which he entered could not but have a happy
tendency to favour his more immediate and compleat preparation for fo fpeedy a remove. To which we may add, that
it muft probably have a very powerful influence to promote
the interefts of religion (incomparably the greateft of all interefts) among the members of his own family; who muft
furely edify much by fuch daily leffons as they received from
his lips, when they faw them illuftrated and enforced by fo
admirable an example, and this for two compleat years. It
is the more remarkable, as I cannot find from the memoirs
of his life in my hands, that he had ever been fo long at
home fince he had a family, or indeed, from his childhood,
ever fo long at a time in any one place.

§. 131. With how clear a luftre his lamp fhone, and with
what holy vigour his loins were girded up in the fervice of
his God, in thefe his latter days, I learn in part from the
letters of feveral excellent perfons in the miniftry, or in fe-
cular life, with whom I have fince converfed or correfpon-
ded. And in his many letters, dated from Bankton during
this period, I have ftill farther evidence, how happy he was,
amidft thofe infirmities of body, which his tendernefs for me
would feldom allow him to mention; for it appears from
them, what a daily intercourfe he kept up with heaven, and
what delightful communion with God crowned his at'en-
dance on public ordinances, and his fweet hours of devout
retirement. He mentions his facramental opportunities
with peculiar relifh, crying out as in a holy rapture. in reference to one and another of them, " Oh how gracious a
" mafter do we ferve! How pleafant is his fervice! How
" rich the entertainments of his love! Yet, Oh how poor,

" and cold, are our fervices!"—But I will not multiply quotations of this fort, after thofe I have given above, which may be a fufficient fpecimen of many more in the fame ftrain. This hint may fuffice to fhew, that the fame ardor of foul held out in a great meafure to the laft; and indeed it feems, that towards the clofe of life, like the flame of a lamp almoft expiring, it fometimes exerted an unufual blaze.

§. 132. He fpent much of his time at Bankton in religious folitude; and one moft intimately converfant with him affures me, that the traces of that delightful converfe with God which he enjoyed in it, might eafily be difcerned in that folemn yet chearful countenance, with which he often came out of his clofet. Yet his exercifes there muft fometimes have been very mournful, confidering the melancholy views which he had of the ftate of our public affairs. " I " fhould be glad," fays he, (in a letter which he fent me, about the clofe of the year 1743,) " to hear what wife and " good people among you think of the prefent circumftances " of things. For my own part, though I thank God I fear " nothing for myfelf, my apprehenfions for the public are " very gloomy, confidering the deplorable prevalency of al- " moft all kinds of wickednefs amongft us; the natural con- " fequence of the contempt of the gofpel. I am daily of- " fering my prayers to God for this finful land of ours, over " which his judgments feem to be gathering; and my " ftrength is fometimes fo exhaufted with thofe ftrong cries " and tears, which I pour out before God on this occafion, that " I am hardly able to ftand when I arife from my knees." If we have many remaining to ftand in the breach with equal fervency, I hope, crying as our provocations are, God will ftill be intreated for us, and fave us.

§. 133. Moft of the other letters I had the pleafure of receiving from him after our laft feparation, are either filled, like thofe of former years, with tender expreffions of affectionate folicitude for my domeftic comfort and public ufefulnefs, or relate to the writings I publifhed during this time, or to the affairs of his eldeft fon then under my care. But thefe are things, which are by no means of a nature to be communicated here. It is enough to remark in the general, that the Chriftian was ftill mingled with all the care of the friend, and the parent.

§. 134. But I think it incumbent upon me to obſerve, that during this time, and ſome preceding years, his attention, e-ver wakeful to ſuch concerns, was much engaged by ſome religious appearances, which happened about this time, both in England and Scotland; with regard to which ſome may be curious to know his ſentiments. He communicated them to me with the moſt unreſerved freedom; and I cannot ap-prehend myſelf under any engagements to conceal them, as I am perſuaded that it will be no prejudice to his memory that they ſhould be publicly known.

§. 135. It was from Colonel Gardiner's pen that I receiv-ed the firſt notice of that ever memorable ſcene which was opened at Kilſyth, under the miniſtry of the Rev. Mr. Mac-Culloch, in the month of February, 1741-2. He commu-nicated to me the copy of two letters from that eminently favoured ſervant of God, giving an account of that extraor-dinary ſucceſs, which had within a few days accompanied his preaching; when, as I remember, in a little more than a fortnight a hundred and thirty ſouls, who had before con-tinued in long inſenſibility under the faithful preaching of the goſpel, were awakened on a ſudden to attend to it, as if it had been a new revelation brought down from heaven, and atteſted by as aſtoniſhing miracles as ever were wrought by Peter or Paul; though they heard it only from a perſon under whoſe miniſtry they had ſat for ſeveral years. Struck with a power and majeſty in the word of God, which they had never felt before, they crouded his houſe night and day, making their applications to him for ſpiritual direction and aſſiſtance, with an earneſtneſs and ſolicitude, which floods of tears and cries, that ſwallowed up their own words and his, could not ſufficiently expreſs. The Colonel mentioned this at firſt to me, " as matter of eternal praiſe, which he knew " would rejoice my very ſoul:" And when he ſaw it ſpread in the neighbouring parts, and obſerved the glorious refor-mation which it produced in the lives of great multitudes, and the abiding fruits of it for ſucceeding months and years, it increaſed and confirmed his joy. But the facts relating to this matter have been laid before the world in ſo authentic a manner, and the agency of divine grace in them has been ſo rationally vindicated, and ſo pathetically repreſented, in what the reverend and judicious Mr. Webſter has written upon that ſubject, that it is altogether ſuperfluous for me to add any thing farther than my hearty prayers, that the work may be as extensive, as it was apparently glorious and divine.

§. 136. It was with great pleasure that he received any intelligence of a like kind from England; whether the clergy of the established church, or dissenting ministers, whether our own countrymen, or foreigners, were the instruments of it. And whatever weaknesses or errors might mingle themselves with valuable qualities in such as were active in such a work, he appeared to love and honor them, in proportion to the degree he saw reason to believe their hearts were devoted to the service of Christ, and their attempts owned and succeeded by him. I remember, that mentioning one of these gentlemen, who had been remarkably successful in his ministry, and seemed to have met with some very unkind usage, he says, " I had rather be that " despised persecuted man, to be an instrument in the hand " of the Spirit, in converting so many souls, and building " up so many in their holy faith, than I would be empe- " ror of the whole world." Yet this steady and judicious christian, (for such he most assuredly was,) at the same time that he esteemed a man for his good intention and his worthy qualities, did not suffer himself to be hurried away into all the singularity of his sentiments, or to admire his imprudences or excesses. On the contrary, he saw and lamented that artifice, which the great father of fraud has so long and so successfully been practising; who, like the enemies of Israel, when he cannot entirely prevent the building of God's temple, does as it were offer his assistance to carry on the work, that he may thereby get the most effectual opportunities of obstructing it. The Colonel often expressed his astonishment at the wide extremes into which some, whom on the whole he thought very worthy men, were permitted to run in many doctrinal and speculative points; and discerned how evidently it appeared from hence, that we cannot argue the truth of any doctrine from the success of the preacher; since this would be a kind of demonstration, (if I may be allowed the expression) which might equally prove both parts of a contradiction. Yet when he observed, that an high regard to the atonement and righteousness of Christ, and to the free grace of God in him,

I

exerted by the operation of the divine Spirit, was generally common to all who had been peculiarly successful in the conversion and reformation of men, (how widely foever their judgments might differ in other points, and how warmly foever they might oppose each other in consequence of that diverfity ;) it tended greatly to confirm his faith in thefe principles, as well as to open his heart in love to all of every denomination, who maintained an affectionate regard to them.   And though what he remarked as to the conduct and fuccefs of minifters of the moſt oppofite ſtrains of preaching, confirmed him in thefe fentiments; yet he always efteemed and loved virtuous and benevolent men, even where he thought them moſt miſtaken in the notions they formed of religion, or in the methods by which they attempted to ferve it.

§. 137. While I thus reprefent what all who knew him muſt foon have obferved of Colonel Gardiner's affectionate regard to thefe peculiar doctrines of our holy religion, it is neceffary that I fhould alfo inform my reader, that it was not his judgment, that the attention of minifters or their hearers fhould be wholly ingroffed by thefe, excellent as they are ; but that all the parts of the fcheme of truth and duty fhould be regarded in their due connection and proportion.   Far from that diſtempered tafte which can bear nothing but cordials, it was his deliberate judgment, that the law fhould be preached, as well as the gofpel ; and hardly any thing gave him greater offence, than the irreverent manner in which fome, who have been ignorantly extolled as the moſt zealous and evangelical preachers, have fometimes been tempted to fpeak of the former; much indeed to the fcandal of all confiſtent and judicious chriſtians.   He delighted to be inſtructed in his duty, and to hear much of the inward exercifes of the fpiritual and divine life.   And he always wifhed, fo far as I could obferve, to have thefe topics treated in a rational as well as a fpiritual manner, with folidity and order of thought, with perfpicuity and weight of expreffion; as well knowing, that religion is a moſt reafonable fervice ; that God has not chofen idiots or lunaticks as the inftruments, or nonfenfe as the means, of building up his church ; and that though the charge of enthufiafm is often fixed on chriftianity and its minifters, in a wild, undeferved, and indeed (on the whole) enthufi-

aftical manner, by fome of the loudeft or moft folemn pre-
tenders to reafon; yet there is really fuch a thing as enthufiafm, againft which it becomes the true friends of revelation to be diligently on their guard; left chriftianity, inftead
of being exalted, fhould be greatly corrupted and debafed,
and all manner of abfurdity, both in doctrine and practice,
introduced by methods, which (like perfecution,) throw
truth and falfehood on a level, and render the groffeft errors at once more plaufible, and more incurable. He had
too much candour and equity, to fix general charges of this
nature; but he was really (and I think not vainly) appre-
henfive that the emiffaries and agents of the moft corrupt
church that ever difhonored the chriftian name, (by which,
it will eafily be underftood, I mean that of Rome,) might
very poffibly infinuate themfelves into focieties, to which
they could no otherwife have accefs, and make their advantage of that total refignation of the underftanding, and contempt of reafon and learning, which nothing but ignorance,
delirium, or knavery can dictate, to lead men blindfold
whither it pleafed, till it fet them down at the foot of an
altar, where tranfubftantiation itfelf is confecrated.

§. 138. I know not where I can more properly introduce
another part of the Colonel's character, which, obvious as
it was, I have not yet touched upon; I mean, his tendernefs to thofe who were under any fpiritual diftrefs; wherein
he was indeed an example to minifters, in a duty more peculiarly theirs. I have feen many amiable inftances of this
myfelf; and I have been informed of many others: One
of which happened about the time of that awakening in the
weftern parts of Scotland, which I touched upon above;
when the reverend Mr. Mac-Laurin, of Glafgow, found occafion to witnefs to the great propriety, judgment, and felicity of manner, with which he addreffed fpiritual confola-
tion to an afflicted foul, who applied to the profeffor, at a
time when he had not an opportunity immediately to give
audience to the cafe. And indeed as long ago as the year
1726, I find him writing to a friend in a ftrain of tendernefs
in this regard, which might well have become the moft affectionate and experienced paftor. He there congratulates
him on fome religious enjoyments lately received, (in part,
it feems, by his means,) when among others, he has this
modeft expreffion; "If I have been made any way the

" means of doing you good, give the whole glory to God ;
" for he has been willing to ſhew, that the power was en-
" tirely of himſelf, ſi ce he has been pleaſed to make uſe of
" ſo very weak an inſtrument." In the ſame letter he ad-
moniſhes his friend, that he ſhould not be too much ſurpri-
ſed, if after having been (as he expreſſes it,) upon the mount,
he ſhould be brought into the valley again; and reminds
him, that " we live by faith, and not by ſenſible aſſur-
" ance," repreſenting, that there are ſome ſuch full communications from God as ſeem almoſt to ſwallow up the
actings of faith, from whence they take their riſe : " Wher.-
" as when a chriſtian who walks in darkneſs and ſees
" no light, will yet hang (as it were) on the report of an
" abſent Jeſus, and." as one expreſſes it, in alluſion to the
ſtory of Jacob and Joſeph, " can put himſelf as on the cha-
" riot of the promiſes, to be borne on to him, whom now
" he ſees not ; there may be ſublimer and more acceptable
" actings of a pure and ſtrong faith, than in moments
" which afford the ſoul a much more rapturous delight."
This is the ſubſtance of what he ſays in this excellent letter. Some of the phraſes made uſe of might not perhaps be
intelligible to ſeveral of my readers, for which reaſon I do
not exactly tranſcribe them all : But this is plainly and fully his meaning, and moſt of the words are his own.
The ſentiment is ſurely very juſt and important ; and happy would it be for many excellent perſons, who through
wrong notions of the nature of faith (which was never more
miſrepreſented, than now among ſome,) are perplexing
themſelves with moſt groundleſs doubts and ſcruples, if it
were more generally underſtood, admitted, and conſider-
ed.

§. 139. An endeared friend, who was moſt intimately
converſant with the colonel during the two laſt years of his
life, has favoured me with an account of ſome little circumſtances relating to him ; which I eſteem as precious frag-
ments, by which the conſiſtent tenor of his character may
be farther illuſtrated. I ſhall therefore inſert them here,
without being very ſolicitous as to the order in which they
are introduced.

§ 140. He perceived himſelf evidently in a very declining ſtate from his firſt arrival in Britain, and ſeemed to entertain a fixed apprehenſion, that he ſhould continue but a

little while longer in life. " He expected death," says my
good correspondent, " and was delighted with the prospect,"
which did not grow less amiable by a nearer approach. The
word of God, with which he had as intimate an acquaintance as most men I ever knew, and on which (especially on
the New-Testament,) I have heard him make many very
judicious and accurate remarks, was still his daily study ;
and it furnished him with matter of frequent conversation,
much to the edification and comfort of those that were about
him. It was recollected, that among other passages he had
lately spoken of the following, as having made a deep impression on his mind ! " My soul, wait thou only upon God!"
He would repeat it again and again, only, only, only ! So
plainly did he see, and so deeply did he feel, the vanity of
creature confidences and expectations. With the strongest
attestation would he often mention those words in Isaiah, as
verified by long experience : " Thou wilt keep him in perfect
peace, whose mind is stayed on thee ; because he trusteth
in thee." And with peculiar satisfaction would he utter these
heroic words in Habakkuk, which he found armour of proof
against every fear and every contingency : " Though the
fig-tree shall not blossom, neither shall fruit be in the vines ;
the labour of the olive shall fail, and the fields shall yield no
meat ; the flocks shall be cut off from the fold, and there
shall be no herd in the stalls : Yet I will rejoice in the
Lord, I will joy in the God of my salvation." The cxlvth
Psalm was also spoken of by him with great delight, and
Dr. Watts's version of it ; as well as several other of that
excellent person's poetical compofures. My friend, who
transmits to me this account, adds the following words ;
which I desire to insert with the deepest sentiments of unfeigned humility and self-abasement before God, as most
unworthy the honour of contributing in the least degree to
the joys and graces of one so much my superior in every
part of the christian character. " As the joy with which
" good men see the happy fruits of their labours, makes a
" part of the present reward of the servants of God and the
" friends of Jesus, it must not be omitted, even in a letter
" to you, that your spiritual hymns were among his most
" delightful and soul improving repasts ; particularly those,
" on beholding transgressors with grief, and Christ's mef-

" ſage." What is added concerning my book of the riſe
and progreſs of religion, and the terms in which he expreſſed his eſteem of it, I cannot ſuffer to paſs my pen ; only
deſire moſt ſincerely to bleſs God, that eſpecially by the laſt
chapters of that treatiſe, I had an opportunity at ſo great a
diſtance of exhibiting ſome offices of chriſtian friendſhip to
this excellent perſon, in the cloſing ſcenes of life ; which
it would have been my greateſt joy to have performed in
perſon, had providence permitted me then to have been near
him.

§. 141. The former of thoſe hymns my correſpondent
mentions, as having been ſo agreeable to Colonel Gardiner,
I have given the reader above, at the end of Sect. 101.
The latter, which is called **Chriſt's** meſſage, took its riſe
from Luke iv. 18, and ſeq. and is as follows.

I.

Hark ! the glad ſound ! The Saviour comes,
   The Saviour promis'd long !
Let ev'ry heart prepare a throne,
   And ev'ry voice a ſong.

II.

On him the Spirit largely pour'd
   Exerts its ſacred fire :
Wiſdom, and might, and zeal, and love,
   His holy breaſt inſpire.

III.

He comes, the priſoners to releaſe
   In Satan's bondage held :
The gates of braſs before him burſt,
   The iron fetters yield.

IV.

He comes from thickeſt films of vice
   To clear the mental ray,
And on the eye-balls of the blind
   To pour celeſtial day.*

V.

He comes, the broken heart to bind,
   The bleeding ſoul to cure ;
And with the treaſures of his grace
   T' inrich the humble poor.

* This Stanza is moſtly borrowed from Mr. Pope.

VI.

His filver trumpets publifh loud
The jub'lee of the Lord ;
Our debts are all remitted now,
Our heritage reftor'd.

VII.

Our glad hofannahs, Prince of peace,
Thy welcome fhall proclaim ;
And heaven's eternal arches ring
With thy beloved name.

§. 142. There is one hymn more I fhall beg leave to add, plain as it is, which Colonel Gardiner has been heard to mention with particular regard, as expreffing the inmoft fentiments of his foul, and they were undoubtedly fo, in the laft rational moments of his expiring life. It is called, Chrift precious to the believer ; and was compofed to be fung after a fermon on 1 Pet. ii. 7.

I.

Jefus ! I love thy charming name,
'Tis mufic to my ear :
Fain would I found it out fo loud,
That earth and heav'n fhould hear.

II.

Yes, Thou art precious to my foul,
My tranfport, and my truft :
Jewels to thee are gaudy toys,
And gold is fordid duft.

III.

All my capacious pow'rs can wifh,
In thee moft richly meet :
Nor to my eyes is life fo dear,
Nor friendfhip half fo fweet.

IV.

Thy grace ftill dwells upon my heart,
And fheds its fragrance there ;
The nobleft balm of all its wounds,
The cordial of its care.

V.

I'll fpeak the honours of thy name
With my laft lab'ring breath ;
Then fpeechlefs clafp thee in my arms,
The antidote of death.

§. 143 Thoſe who were intimate with Colonel Gardiner muſt have obſerved, how ready he was to give a devotional turn to any ſubject that occurred. And in particular,
the ſpiritual and heavenly diſpoſition of his ſoul diſcovered
itſelf in the reflections and improvements which he made
when reading hiſtory; in which he took a great deal of
pleaſure, as perſons remarkable for their knowledge of mankind, and obſervation of providence, generally do. I have
an inſtance of this before me, which, though too natural
to be at all ſurprizing, will I dare ſay be pleaſing to the devout mind. He had juſt been reading, in Rollin's extract
from Xenophon, the anſwer which the lady of Tigranes
made, when all the company were extolling Cyrus, and
expreſſing the admiration with which his appearance and
behaviour ſtruck them; the queſtion being aſked her, what
ſhe thought of him? She anſwered, I don't know, I did
not obſerve him. On what then, ſaid one of the company,
did you fix your attention? On him, replied ſhe, (referring
to the generous ſpeech which her huſband had juſt made,)
who ſaid he would give a thouſand lives to ranſom my liberty. "Oh," cried the colonel when reading it, "how
" ought we to fix our eyes and hearts on him, who not in
" offer, but in reality, gave his own precious life to ranſom
" us from the moſt dreadful ſlavery, and from eternal de-
" ſtruction!" But this is only one inſtance among a thouſand. His heart was ſo habitually ſet upon divine things,
and he had ſuch a permanent and overflowing ſenſe of the
love of Chriſt, that he could not forbear connecting ſuch
reflections, with a multitude of more diſtant occaſions occurring in daily life, where leſs advanced chriſtians would
not have thought of them: And thus, like our great maſter, he made every little incident a ſource of devotion, and
an inſtrument of holy zeal.

§. 144. Enfeebled as his conſtitution was, he was ſtill
intent on improving his time to ſome valuable purpoſes:
And when his friends expoſtulated with him, that he gave
his body ſo little reſt, he uſed to anſwer, " It will reſt long
" enough in the grave."

§. 145. The July before his death, he was perſuaded to
take a journey to Scarborough for the recovery of his health;
from which he was at leaſt encouraged to expect ſome little
revival. After this he had thoughts of going to London,

and defigned to have fpent part of September ber at Northampton. The expectation of this was mutually agreeable; but providence faw fit to difc ncern the fcheme. His love for his friends in thefe parts occafioned him to exprefs fome re. gret on his being commanded back: And I am pretty confident, from the manner in which he exprefled himfelt in one of his laft letters to me, that he had fome more important reafons for wifning an opportunity of making a London journey juft at that crifis; which, the reader will remember, was before the rebellion broke out. But as providence determined it otherwife, he acquiefced; and I am well fatisfied that could he have diftinctly forefeen the approaching event, fo far as it concerned his own perfon, he would have efteemed it the happieft fummons he ever received While he was at Scarborough, I find by a letter dated from thence, July 26, 1745, that he had been informed of the gaiety which fo unfeafonably prevailed at Edinburgh, where great multitudes were then fpending their time in balls, affemblies, and other gay amufements, little mindful of the rod of God which was then hanging over them: on which occafion he hath this expreffion: "I am greatly furprized, that the " people of Edinburgh fhould be employed in fuch foolifh " diverfions, when our fituation is at prefent more melan- " choly than ever I faw it in my life. But there is one " thing which I am very fure of, that comforts me, viz. " that it fhall go well with the righteous, come what will."

§. 146. Quickly after his return home, the flame burft out, and his regiment was ordered to Stirling. It was in the caftle there that his lady and eldeft daughter'enjoyed the laft happy hours of his company; and I think, it was about eight or ten days before his death, that he parted from them there. A remarkable circumftance attended that parting, which hath been touched upon by furviving friends in more then one of their letters to me. His lady was fo affected when fhe took her laft leave of him, that fhe could not forbear burfting out into a flood of tears, with other marks of unufual emotion. And when he afked her the reafon, fhe urged the apprehenfion fhe had of lofing fuch an invaluable friend, amidft the dangers to which he was then called out, as a very fufficient apology. Upon which fhe took particular notice, that whereas he had generally comforted her on fuch occafions, by pleading with

her that remarkable hand of providence, which had ſo frequently in former inſtances being exerted for his preſerva-
tion, and that in the greateſt extremity, he ſaid nothing
of it now; but only replied, in his ſententious manner,
"We have an eternity to ſpend together."

§. 147. That heroic contempt of death which had often diſcovered itſelf in the midſt of former dangers, was
manifeſted now in his diſcourſe with ſeveral of his moſt intimate friends. I have reſerved for this place one genuine
expreſſion of it many years before, which I thought might
be mentioned with ſome advantage here, In July, 1725,
he had been ſent to ſome place, not far from Hamilton, to
quell a mutiny among ſome of our troops. I know not the
particular occaſion; but I remember to have heard him mention it as ſo fierce a one, that he ſcarce ever apprehended
himſelf in a more hazardous circumſtance. Yet he quelled
it, by his preſence alone, and the expoſtulations he uſed; e-
vidently putting his life into his hand to do it. The particulars of the ſtory ſtruck me much; but I do not ſo exactly remember them, as to venture to relate them here. I only obſerve, that in a letter dated July 16, that year, which
I have now before me, and which evidently refers to this
event, he writes thus: "I have been very buſy, hurried
"about from place to place; but bleſſed be God, all is over
"without bloodſhed And pray let me aſk, what made
"you ſhow ſo much concern for me in your laſt? Were
"you afraid, I ſhould get to heaven before you? Or can
"any evil befall thoſe, who are followers of that which is
"good?" *

---

* I doubt not, but this will remind ſome of my readers of that
noble ſpeech of Zuinglius, when (according to the uſage of that
country,) attending his flock to a battle in which their religion
and liberties were all at ſtake, on his receiving a mortal wound
by a bullet, of which he ſoon expired, while his friends were in
all the ſir aſtoniſhment of grief, he bravely ſaid as he was dying, "Ecquid hoc infortunii? Is this to be reckoned a misfor-
"tune?" How many of our deiſts would have celebrated ſuch
a ſentence, if it had come from the lips of an ancient Roman?
ſtrange, that the name of Chriſt ſhould be ſo odious, that the
brighteſt virtues of his followers ſhould be deſpiſed for his ſake!
But ſo it is; and ſo our maſter told us, it would be: And our
faith is in this connection confirmed by thoſe, that ſtrive moſt to
overthrow it.

§. 148. And as thefe were his fentiments in the vigour of his days, fo neither did declining years and the infirmities of a broken conftitution on the one hand, nor any defires of enjoying the honours and profits of fo high a ftation, or (what was much more to him,) the converfe of the moft affectionate of wives and fo many amiable children and friends on the other, enervate his fpirits in the leaft : But as he had in former years often expreffed it, to me and feveral others, as his defire, " that if it were the will of " God, he might have fome honourable call to facrifice his " life in defence of religion and the liberties of his country ;" fo when it appeared to him moft probable that he might be called to it immediately, he met the fummons with the greateft readinefs.   This appears in part from a letter which he wrote to the reverend Mr. Adams of Falkirk, juft as he was on marching from Stirling, which was only eight days before his death : " The rebels," fays he, are " advancing " to crofs the Firth ; but I truft in the Almighty God, who " doth whatfoever he pleafes, in the armies of heaven, and " among the inhabitants of the earth."   And the fame gentleman tells me, that a few days after the date of this, he marched through Falkirk with his regiment ; and though he was then in fo languifhing a ftate, that he needed his affiftance as a fecretary to write for fome reinforcement, which might put it in his power to make a ftand, (as he was very defirous to have done,) he expreffed a moft genuine and noble contempt of life, when to be expofed in the defence of a worthy caufe.

§. 149. Thefe fentiments wrought in him to the laft, in the moft effectual manner ; and he feemed for a while to have infufed them into the regiment which he commanded : For they expreffed fuch a fpirit in their march from Stirling, that I am affured, the colonel was obliged to exert all his authority to prevent their making incurfions on that rebel army, which then lay very near them ; and had it been thought proper to fend him the reinforcement he requefted, none can fay what the confequence might have been.   But he was ordered to march as faft as poffible, to meet Sir John Cope's forces at Dunbar ; which he did : And that hafty retreat, in concurrence with the news which they foon after received of the furrender of Edinburgh to the rebels, (either by the treachery or weaknefs of a few, in oppofition to the judgment of by far the greater and better part of the inhabitants,) struck a panic into both of the regiments of dragoons, which became visible in some very apparent and remarkable circumstances in their behaviour, when I forbear to relate. This affected Colonel Gardiner so much, that on the Thursday before the fatal action at Preston-Pans, he intimated to an officer of considerable rank and note, (from whom I had it by a very sure channel of conveyance,) that he expected the event would be, as in fact it was. In this view, there is all imaginable reason to believe, he had formed his resolution as to his own personal conduct, which was, "that he " would not, in case of the flight of those under his command, " retreat with them;" by which, as it seemed, he was reasonably apprehensive, he might have stained the honour of his former services, and have given some occasion for the enemy to have spoken reproachfully. He much rather chose, if providence gave him the call, to leave in his death an example of fidelity and bravery, which might very probably be (as in fact it seems indeed to have been,) of much greater importance to his country, than any other service, which in the few days of remaining life he could expect to render it. I conclude these to have been his views, not only from what I knew of his general character and temper, but likewise from some intimations which he gave to a very worthy person from Edinburgh, who visited him the day before the action; to whom he said, "I cannot influence the conduct of others, " as I could wish; but I have one life to sacrifice to my country's safety, and I shall not spare it;" or words to that effect.

§. 150. I have heard such a multitude of inconsistent reports of the circumstances of Colonel Gardiner's death, that I had almost despaired of being able to give my reader any particular satisfaction concerning so interesting a scene. But by a happy accident I have very lately had an opportunity of being exactly informed of the whole, by that brave man Mr. John Foster, his faithful servant, (and worthy of the honor of serving such a master,) whom I had seen with him at my house some years before. He attended him in his last hours, and gave me the narration at large; which he would be ready, were it requisite, to attest upon oath. From his mouth I wrote it down with the utmost exactness, and could easily believe from the genuine and affectionate manner in which he related the particulars, that according to his own

ftriking expreffion, " his eye and his heart were always
" upon his honoured mafter during the whole time."*

§. 151. On Friday, September 20, (the day before the
battle which tranfmitted him to his immortal crown) when
the whole army was drawn up, 1 think about noon, the
Colonel rode through all the ranks of his own regiment ; ad-
dreffing them at once in the moft refpectful and animating
manner, both as foldiers, and as chriftians, to engage them
to exert themfelves couragioufly in the fervice of their country, and to neglect nothing that might have a tendency to
prepare them for whatever event might happen. They feemed much affected with the addrefs, and expreffed a very ardent defire of attacking the enemy immediately : A defire,
in which he and another very gallant officer of diftinguifhed
rank, dignity, and character, both for bravery and conduct, would gladly him gratified them, if it had been in the
power of either. He earneftly preffed it on the commanding officer, both as the foldiers were then in better fpirits,
than it could be fuppofed they would be, after having paffed the night under arms ; and alfo as the circumftance of
making an attack would be fome encouragement to them,
and probably fome terror to the enemy, who would have had
the difadvantage of ftanding on the defence ; a difadvantage, with which thofe wild barbarians (for fuch moft of
them were,) perhaps would have been more ftruck than better difciplined troops : efpecially, when they fought againft
the laws of their country too. He alfo apprehended, that
by marching to meet them, fome advantage might have been
fecured with regard to the ground ; with which, it is natural to imagine, he muft have been perfectly acquainted,
as it lay juft at his own door, and he had rode over it fo many hundred times When I mention thefe things, I do not
pretend to be capable of judging, how far this advice was

K

---

* Juft as I am putting the laft hand to thefe memoirs, March
2, 1746-7, I have met with a corporal in Colonel Lafcelles's re-
gimet, who was alfo an eye-witnefs to what happened at Preft-
on-Pans on the day of the battle, and the day before : And the
account he has given me of fome memorable particulars is fo exactly agreeable to that which I received from Mr. Forfter, that
it would much corroborate his teftimony, if there were not fo
many other confiderations to render it convincing.

on the whole right. A variety of circumſtances, to me unknown, might make it otherwiſe. It is certain however, that it was brave. But it was over-ruled in this reſpeĉt, as it alſo was in the diſpoſition of the cannon, which he would have had planted in the centre of our ſmall army, rather than juſt before his regiment, which was in the right wing; where he was apprehenſive, the horſes, which had not been in any engagement before, might be thrown into ſome diſorder by the diſcharge ſo very near them. He urged this the more, as he thought the attack of the rebels might probably be made on the centre of the foot, where he knew there were ſome brave men, on whoſe ſtanding he thought under God the ſucceſs of the day depended. When he found, that he could not carry either of theſe points, nor ſome others, which out of regard to the common ſafety he inſiſted upon with ſome unuſual earneſtneſs, he dropped ſome intimations of the conſequences which he apprehended, and which did in faĉt follow; and ſubmitting to Providence, ſpent the remainder of the day in making as good a diſpoſition, as circumſtances would allow.*

§ 152. He continued all night under arms, wrapped up in his cloak, and generally ſheltered under a rick of barley, which happened to be in the field. About three in the morning, he called his domeſtic ſervants to him, of which there were four in waiting. He diſmiſſed three of them, with moſt affeĉtionate chriſtian advice, and ſuch ſolemn charges relating to the performance of their duty, and the care of their ſouls, as ſeemed plainly to intimate, that he apprehended it at leaſt very probable, he was taking his laſt farewell of them. There is great reaſon to believe, that he

---

* Several of theſe circumſtances have ſince been confirmed by the concurrent teſtimony of another very credih'e perſen, Mr. R bert Douglas, (now a ſurgeon in the navy,) who was a volunteer at Edinburgh juſt before the rebels entered the place; who ſaw Colonel Gardiner come from Haddington to the field of battle the day before the aĉtion in a chaiſe, being (as from that circumſtance he ſuppoſed.) in ſo weak a ſtate that he could not well endure the fatigue of riding on horſe-back. He obſerved Colonel Gardiner in diſcourſe with ſeveral officers, the evening before the engagement; at which time, it was afterwards reported, he gave his advice to attack the rebels: And when it was over-ruled, he afterwards ſaw the Colonel walk by himſelf in a very penſive manner.

spent the little remainder of the time, which could not be much above an hour, in those devout exercifes of foul, which had fo long been habitual to him, and to which fo many circumftances did then concur to call him. The army was alarmed by break of day, by the noife of the rebels approach, and the attack was made before fun rife; yet when it was light enough to difcern what paffed. As foon as the enemy came within gun-fhot, they made a furious fire; and it is faid, that the dragoons which conftituted the left wing, immediately fled. The Colonel at the beginning of the onfet, which in the whole lafted but a few minutes, received a wound by a bullet in his left breaft, which made him give a fudden fpring on his faddle; upon which his fervant, who had the led horfe, would have perfuaded him to retreat: But he faid, it was only a wound in the flefh; and fought on, though he prefently after received a fhot in his right thigh. In the mean time it was difcerned, that fome of the enemy fell by him; and particularly one man, who had made him a treacherous vifit but a few days before, with great profeffions of zeal for the prefent eftablifhment.

§ 153. Events of this kind pafs in lefs time, than the defcription of them can be written, or than it can be read. The Colonel was for a few moments fupported by his men, and particularly by that worthy perfon, lieutenant-colonel Whitney, who was fhot through the arm here, and a few months after fell nobly in the battle of Falkirk; and by lieutenant Weft, a man of diftinguifhed bravery; as alfo by about fifteen dragoons, who ftood by him to the laft. But after a faint fire, the regiment in general was feized with a pannic; and though their Colonel and fome other gallant officers, did what they could to rally them once or twice, they at laft took a precipitate flight. And juft in the moment when Colonel Gardiner feemed to be making a paufe, to deliberate what duty required him to do in fuch a circumftance, an accident happened, which muft I think, in the judgment of every worthy and generous man, be allowed a fufficient apology for expofing his life to fo great hazard, when his regiment had left him.* He faw a party of the

---

* The Colonel, who was well acqainted with military hiftory, might poffibly remember, that in the battle at Blenheim, the illuftrious Prince Eugene, when the horfe of the wing he commanded had run away thrice, charged at the head of the foot,

foot, who were then bravely fighting near him, and whom he was ordered to ſupport, had no officer to head them; upon which he ſaid eagerly, in the hearing of the perſon from whom I had this account, " Thoſe brave fellows will be " cut to pieces for want of a commander ;" or words to that effect : Which while he was ſpeaking, he rode up to them, and cried out aloud, " Fire on, my lads, and fear nothing." But juſt as the words were out of his mouth, an Highlander advanced towards him with a ſcythe faſtened to a long pole, with which he gave him ſuch a deep wound on his right arm, that his ſword dropped out of his hand ; and at the ſame time ſeveral others coming about him, while he was thus dreadfully intangled with that cruel weapon, he was dragged off from his horſe. The moment he fell, another Highlander, who, if the king's evidence at Carliſle may be credited, (as I know not why they ſhould not, though the unhappy creature died denying it,) was one Mac-naught, who was executed about a year after, gave him a ſtroke, either with a broad-ſword, or a Lochabar axe, (for my informant could not exactly diſtinguiſh,) on the hinder part of his head, which was the mortal blow. All that his faithful attendant ſaw farther at this time was, that as his hat was fallen off, he took it in his left hand, and waved it as a ſignal to him to retreat ; and added, what were the laſt words he ever heard him ſpeak, " Take care of yourſelf :" Upon which the ſervant retired.

§. 154. It was reported at Edinburgh on the day of the battle, by what ſeemed a conſiderable authority, that as the Colonel lay in his wounds, he ſaid to a chief of the oppoſite ſide, " You are fighting for an earthly crown, I am going " to receive an heavenly one ;" or ſomething to that purpoſe. When I preached the ſermon, long ſince printed, on occaſion of his death, I had great reaſon to believe, this report was true ; though before the publication of it I began

and thereby greatly contributed to the glorious ſucceſs of the day. At leaſt ſuch an example may conduce to vindicate that noble ardour, which, amidſt all the applauſes of his country, ſome have been ſo cool and ſo critical as to blame. For my own part, I thank God, that I am not called to apologize for his following his troops in their flight ; which I fear would have been a much harder taſk ; and which, dear as he was to me, would have grieved me much more than his death, with theſe heroic circumſtances attending it.

to be in doubt : And on the whole, after the moft accurate enquiry I could poffibly make at this diftance, I cannot get any convincing evidence of it. Yet I muft here obferve, that it does not appear impoffible, that fomething of this kind might indeed be uttered by him ; as his fervant tefti-fies, that he fpoke to him after receiving that fatal blow, which would feem moft likely to have taken away the pow-er of fpeech ; and as it is certain, he lived feveral hours af-ter he fell. If therefore any thing of this kind did happen, it muft have been juft about this inftant. But as to the ſto-ry of his being taken prifoner, and carried to the pretended prince, (who by the way afterwards rode his horfe, and en-tered upon it into Derby) with feveral other circumftances which were grafted upon that interview, there is the moft undoubted evidence of its falfehood. For his attendant men-tioned above, affures me, that he himfelf immediately fled to a mill, at the diftance of about two miles from the fpot of ground on which the Colonel fell ; where he changed his drefs, and, difguifed like a miller's fervant, returned with a cart as foon as poffible ; which yet was not till near two hours after the engagement. The hurry of the action was then pretty well over, and he found his much honored maf-ter, not only plundered of his watch and other things of va-lue, but alfo ftripped of his upper garments and boots ; yet ftill breathing : And adds, that though he were not capable of fpeech, yet on taking him up he opened his eyes ;. which makes it fomething queftionable, whether he were altoge-ther infenfible. In this condition, and in this manner, he conveyed him to the church of Tranent, from whence he was immediately taken into the minifter's houfe, and laid in bed, where he continued breathing, and frequently groan-ing, till about eleven in the forenoon ; when he took his fi-nal leave of pain and forrow, and undoubtedly rofe to thofe diftinguifhed glories, which are referved for thofe who have been fo eminently and remarkably faithful unto death.

§. 155. From the moment in which he fell, it was no longer a battle, but a rout and carnage. The cruelties, which the rebels, (as it is generally faid, under the command of Lord Elcho) inflicted on fome of the king's troops after they had afked quarter, are dreadfully legible on the countenan-ces of many who furvived it. They entered Colonel Gardiner's houſe, before he was carried off from the field ; and, notwithſtanding the ſtrict orders which the unhappy Duke of Perth, (whoſe conduct is ſaid to have been very humane in many inſtances) gave to the contrary, every thing of value was plundered, to the very curtains of the beds, and hangings of the r oms. His papers were all thrown into the wildeſt diſorder, and his houſe made an hoſpital for the reception of thoſe who were wounded in the action.

§. 156 Such was the cloſe of a life, which had been ſo zealouſly devoted to God, and filled up with ſo many honorable ſervices. This was the death of him, who had been ſo highly favoured by God, in the method by which he was brought back to him after ſo long and ſo great an eſtrangement, and in the progreſs of ſo many years, during which (in the expreſſive phraſe of the moſt ancient of writers,) he had walked with him ;—to fall, as God threatened the people of his wrath that they ſhould do, " with tumult, with ſhouting, and with the ſound of the trumpet." (Amos ii. 2.) Several other very worthy, and ſome of them very eminent perſons, ſhared the ſame fate ; either now in the battle of Preſton-Pans or quickly after in that of Falkirk :* Providence, no doubt, permitting it, to eſtabliſh our faith in the rewards of an inviſible world ; as well as to teach us, to ceaſe from man, and fix our dependence on an Almighty arm.

§. 157. The remains of this chriſtian hero (as I believe every reader is now convinced, he may juſtly be called,) were interred the Tueſday following, Sept. 24, at the pariſh church at Tranent, where he had uſually attended divine ſervice with great ſolemnity. His obſequies were honoured with the preſence of ſome perſons of diſtinction, who were not afraid of paying that laſt piece of reſpect to his memory, though the country was then in the hands of the enemy. But indeed there was no great hazard in this ; for his character was ſo well known, that even they themſelves ſpoke honorably of him, and ſeemed to join with his friends in lamenting the fall of ſo brave and ſo worthy a man.

* Of theſe none were more honourable than thoſe illuſtrious brothers, Sir Robert Munro, and Doctor Munro ; whoſe tragical but glorious fate was alſo ſhared quickly after by a third hero of the family, captain Munro of Culcairn, brother to Sir Robert and the Doctor.

§. 158. The remoteſt poſterity will remember, for whom the honour of ſubduing this unnatural and pernicious rebellion was reſerved; and it will endear the perſon of the illuſtrious duke of Cumberland, to all but the open, or ſecret abettors of it in the preſent age, and conſecrate his name to immortal honours among all the friends of religion and liberty who ſhall ariſe after us. And I dare ſay, it will not be imagined, that I at all derogate from his glory, in ſuggeſting, that the memory of that valiant and excellent perſon whoſe memoirs I am now concluding, may in ſome meaſure have contributed to that ſignal and compleat victory, with which God was pleaſed to crown the arms of his royal highneſs: For the force of ſuch an example is very animating, and a painful conſciouſneſs of having deſerted ſuch a commander in ſuch extremity muſt at leaſt awaken, where there was any ſpark of generoſity an earneſt deſire to avenge his death on thoſe, who had ſacrificed his blood, and that of ſo many other excellent perſons, to the views of their ambition, rapine, or bigotry.

§ 159 The reflections I have made in my funeral ſermon on my honoured friend, and in the dedication of it to his worthy and moſt afflicted lady, ſupercede many things which might otherwiſe have properly been added here. I conclude thereore, with humbly acknowledging the wiſdom and goodneſs of that awful providence, which drew ſo thick a gloom around him in the laſt hours of his life, that the luſtre of his virtues might dart through it with a more vivid and obſervable ray. It is abundant matter of thankfulneſs, that ſo ſignal a monument of grace and ornament of the chriſtian profeſſion, was raiſed in our age and country, and ſpared for ſo many honourable and uſeful years Nor can all the tenderneſs of the moſt affectionate friendſhip, while its ſorrows bleed afreſh in the view of ſo tragical a ſcene, prevent my adoring the gracious appointment of the great Lord of all events, that when the day in which he muſt have expired without an enemy appeared ſo very near, the laſt ebb of his generous blood ſhould be poured out, as a kind of ſacred libation, to the liberties of his country, and the honour of his God that all the other virtues of his character, embalmed as it were by that precious ſtream, might diffuſe around a more extenſive fragrancy, and be tranſmitted to the moſt remote poſterity with that peculiar charm, which they cannot but derive from their connection with ſo gallant a fall : An event, (as that bleſſed apoſtle, of whoſe ſpirit he ſo deeply drank, has expreſſed it,) according to his earneſt expectation, and his hope, that in him Chriſt might be glorified in all things whether by his life, or by his death.

A P P E N D I X.

Relating to the COLONEL's Perſon.

IN the midſt of ſo many more important articles, I had really forgot to ſay any thing of the perſon of Colonel Gardiner, of which nevertheleſs it may be proper here to add a word or two. It was, as I am informed, in younger life remarkably graceful and amiable : And I can eaſily believe it, from what I knew him to be, when our acquaintance began ; though he was then turned of fifty, and had gone through ſo many fatigues as well as dangers, which could not but leave ſome traces on his countenance. He was tall, (I ſuppoſe, ſomething more than ſix foot,) well proportioned, and ſtrongly built : His eyes of a dark grey, and not very large ; his forehead pretty high ; his noſe of a length and height no way remarkable, but very well ſuited to his other features ; his cheeks not very prominent, his mouth moderately large, and his chin rather a little inclining (when I knew him) to be peaked. He had a ſtrong voice, and lively accent ; with an air very intriped, yet attempered with much gentleneſs : And there was ſomething in his manner of addreſs moſt perfectly eaſy and obliging, which was in a great meaſure the reſult of the great candor and benevolence, of his natural temper ; and which, no doubt, was much improved by the deep humility which divine grace had wrought into his heart; as well as having been accuſtomed from his early youth, to the company of perſons of diſtinguiſhed rank and polite behaviour.

The picture of him, was taken from an original done by Van Deeſt, (a Dutchman brought into Scotland by general Wade) in the year 1727, which was the 40th of his age ;

and is faid to have been very like him then, though far
from being an exact refemblance of what he was when I had
the happinefs of being acquainted with him. Perhaps he would
have appeared to the greateft advantage of all, could he have
been exactly drawn on horfeback : as many very good judges,
and among the reft the celebrated Monf. Faubert himfelf,
have fpoken of him as one of the compleateft horfemen that
has ever been known : And there was indeed fomething fo
fingularly graceful in his appearance in that attitude, that
it was fufficient (as what is very eminent in its kind generally is,) to ftrike an eye not formed on any critical rules.

POETICAL PIECES on the Death

of *Colonel* GARDINER.

SO animating a fubject as the death of fuch a man, in
fuch circumftances, has occafioned a great deal of poe-
try. Some of this has already been publifhed; efpecially
one large compofition, faid to be done by a worthy clergyman in Lincolnfhire, in which there are many excellent
lines and noble fentiments : But I rather choofe to refer to the
piece itfelf, than to infert any extracts from it here. It
may be more expedient to oblige my reader with the following copy of verfes, and an elegiack poem, compofed by
two of my valuable friends whofe names are annexed. I
could not prefume to attempt any thing of this kind myfelf;
becaufe I knew, that nothing I was capable of writing could
properly exprefs my fenfe of his worth, or defcribe the tendernefs of my friendfhip; the fentiments of which will (as
I affuredly believe,) mingle themfelves with the laft ideas
which pafs through my mind in this world, and perhaps
with fome of the firft which may open upon it in that which
is to come,

Verfes on the Death of *Col. Gardiner.*

By the Rev. Mr. *Benjamin Snowden.*

Quis Defiderio fit Pudor, aut Modus,
Tam chari Capitis ?   HOR.

COULD piety perpetuate human breath,
Or fhield one mortal from the chafts of death,
Thou ne'er, illuftrious man ! thou ne'er hadft been
A pallid corpfe on Prefton's fatal plain.
Or could her hand, though impotent to fave
Confummate worth, redeem it from the grave,
Soon would thy urn refign its facred truft,
And recent life re-animate thy duft.
But vain the wifh.—The favage hand of war—
Oh how fhall words the mournful tale declare !

Too foon the news afflicted friendfhip hears,
Too foon, alas, confirm'd her boding fears.
  Struck with the found, unconfcious of redrefs,
She felt thy wounds, and wept fevere diftrefs,
A while diffolv'd in trucelefs grief fhe lay,
And mourn'd th' event of that unhappy day;
Which lett thee to rentlefs rage a prey.
  At length kind fame fufpends our heaving fighs,
And wipes the forrows from our flowing eyes ;
Gives us to know, thine exit well fupply'd
Thofe blooming laurels victory deny'd.
When thy great foul fupprefs'd each timid moan,
And foar'd triumphant in a dying groan,
Thy fall, which rais'd, now calms each wild complaint,
Thy fall, which join'd the hero to the faint.
  As o'er th' expiring lamp the quiv'ring flame
Collects its luftre in a brighter gleam,
Thy virtues, glimm'ring on the verge of night,
Through the dim fhade diffus'd celeftial light ;
A radiance, death or time can ne'er deftroy,
Th' aufpicious omen of eternal joy.
  Hence ev'ry unavailing grief ! No more
As haplefs thy removal we deplore.
Thy gufhing veins, in every drop they bleed,
Of patriot warrors fhed the fruitful feed.
Soon fhall the ripen'd harveft rife in arms
To crufh rebellion's infolent alarms.
  While profp'rous moments footh'd through life his way,
Conceal'd from public view the hero lay :
But when affliction clouded his decline,
Is not eclips'd, but made his honours fhine ;
Gave them to beam confpicuous from the gloom,
And plant unfading trophies round his tomb.
  So ftars are loft, amidft the blaze of day ;
But when the fun withdraws his golden ray,
Refulgent through th' ætherial arch they roll,
And gild the wide expanfe from pole to pole.

An ELEGY

On the Death of the truly pious and brave

Col. *JAMES GARDINER,*

Who was flain by the Rebel Forces, September 21, 1745,

In the fatal Action at Preston-Pans.

By the Rev. Mr. Thomas Gibbons.

> *Nam, dum Duelli lætior, hoftica*
> *Opprobriorum Murmura vindice*
> *Excufat Enfe, barbararum*
> *Immortuus Aggeribus Cohortum;*
> *Præfecta tandem Colla volubili*
> *Lapfu reclinat. Sed famula prope*
> *Decufque, præfignifque Virtus,*
> *Semtanimem fubiere Dextra:*
> *Mox, expedites Corpore Manibus,*
> *Depræliatrix Gloria Siderum*
> *Occurrit, et fulvo, reclinem*
> *Ire jubet fuper A ftra Curru.*
>
> Casimir.

I.

COME, Melancholy, from the ftony cave
The fcoop of Time for thee has made
    Under the broad cliff's fhade,
    Upon the naked fhore,
    Where warring tempefts roar
In concert with the hoarfe refounding wave!
    Come, but with folemn gait,
      With trickling eyes,
      And heavy fighs,
    And all the 'fcutcheon'd pomp of fate;
And bring with thee the cyprefs, and the yew,
All bath'd and dropping with the mortal dew,
      To this fequefter'd bow'r;
    And let the midnight hour
Be hung in deeper glooms by thee,
And bid each gay idea flee:

While all the baleful images of woe,
   That haunt the marble buſt,
   Or hover round ſepulcher'd duſt,
With conſcious horrors all my ſoul o'erflow.
   For 'tis no vulgar death
   Urania means to mourn ;
   But in a doleful ſtrain
   She bids the harp complain,
   And hangs the fun'ral wreath
   On Gard'ner's awful urn.

II.

   Gard'ner, what various fame
   For ever crowns thy name ?
Nor is it poſſible to ſay.
Or if the ſaint's, or hero's ray
Shone brighteſt in that blended blaze,
That form'd thine ample round of praiſe.
Like Moſes on the ſacred hill,
How haſt thou ſtood with pleading eyes,
Out-ſtretching hands, and fervent cries,
   Unwearied wreſtler with the ſkies ?
   Till heav'n, reſponſive to thy will,
   Would all thy largeſt wiſhes fill ;
Till the high brandiſh'd bolt aſide was thrown,
And the full bleſſing ſtream'd in ſilver murmurs down.
   Nor leſs a joſhua, than a Moſes, thou ;
   For oft in liberty's high ſtrife
   Haſt thou expos'd thy gen'rous life,
   And with impatient ardours on thy brow,
   Ruſh'd foremoſt in the horrid van of fight,
   Driving the troops of tyranny to flight,
   Unſhaken in the noble cauſe
To pluck her bloody fangs, and break her iron jaws.

III.

   When Anna ſent her choſen chief,
      Victorious Marlborough,
   To Europe's groans to give relief,
      In Bourbon's overthrow :
   Renown'd Ramilia's tented field,
   Where Gallia dropt her idle ſhield
   And to the Britiſh ſtandard kneel'd,

L

Beheld young Gard'ner there.
Young Gard'ner, where the combat mow'd
The falling ranks, and widely ftrow'd
    Deftruction and defpair,
Wielded ferene his youthful arms,
And, kindling at the dire alarms,
    Enjoy'd the raging war :
But here, (for fteel and flying fhot,
Fall chiefly to the hero's lot,)
Swift through his lips the glancing bullet rung,
His lips, on which th' unfinifh'd oath was hung;
    Nor ftopt its wing'd impetuous force
Till through the neck it plough'd its angry courfe.
Amazing thought ! that they who life expofe,
Where all the thunder of the battle glows,
    Who fee pale death triumphant ride
    Upon the crimfon's furging tide,
    Scatt'ring his chafts on ev'ry fide,
In blafphemy and proud contempt fhould rife,
And hurl their mad defiance to the fkies ;
    Whither a moment may convey
Their fouls, diflodging from their quiv'ring clay,
To take their laft inexorable doom,
Big with immortal wrath, and dire defpair to come.

IV.

Such Gard'ner was in early youth :
    And while the warrior's rays
Beam'd round his head, celeftial truth
    He fpurn'd, and fcorn'd her ways :
And, though th' Almighty arm was near,
Made his endanger'd life its care,
    And heal'd the burning fores ;
Yet vice, collecting with his ftrength,
Soon, foon burfts out in wilder length,
    And like a torrent roars.
Now in the wide enchanting bowl
The hero melts his manly foul ;
And now he boits the fhades of night.
With blacker fcenes of lewd delight:
Anon in fport he lifts his brow to heav'n,
    And fwares by the eternal name ;
Afks that the bolt may on his head be driven,

And courts the lagging flame.
So Pharaoh, when the fev'r th blains
    No more embofs'd his flesh,
Nor fhot infection through his veins,
    Affum'd his rage a frefh;
And hard, grew harder ftill,
And prop'd on his wild will,
Set up the flandard of his pride,
Curft Ifr'els God and king, and all his plagues defy'd,
                    V.
But, mufe, in fofter notes relate,
For fofter notes upon thee wait,
How Gard'ner, when his youth had rang'd
Thefe guilty fcenes, to heav'n eftrang'd,
Paus'd in his mid career, and was divinely chang'd.
That God, whofe piercing radiance darts
O'er all our ways, and all our hearts,
The bold tranfgreffor from his throne furvey'd,
And thus in accents breathing mildnefs faid:
" Go, Mercy, charg'd with my fupreme command,
" Thou faireft daughter thron'd at my right hand,
        " Go, wing thy downward race,
" And ftop that rebel in his furious way;
" His heart fhall thy victorious call obey,
    " And take the willing ftamp of grace:
" For never fhall thy call fuccefslefs prove,
    " And thou lament thy baffled aim,
    " If thou but dart thy chofen flame,
" Arm'd with the Saviour's energy of love."
He fpoke; and gave th' Almighty nod,
The fanction of th' eternal God:
At once the joyful news is propagated round,
Loud anthems from the golden roofs rebound,
And heav'ns high cryftal domes remurmur with the found.
                    VI.
Mercy obeys; and from th' empyreal height
    Precipitates her glitt'ring flight;
A ftarry circle fparkled round her head,
And a wide rainbow o'er her progrefs fpread.
    Mufe, fing the wond'rous plan,
    And fing the wond'rous hour,
    In which the Sov'reign Pow'r

Th' Almighty work began,
And fignaliz'd her arm, and triumph'd o'er the man.
Bent on adult'rous fhame
The finner fhe beheld;
His bofom burnt with guilty flame,
And at the future joy in fecret raptures fwell'd:
Enrag'd he curs'd the lazy moon
In her nocturnal tour
That thought his blifs would come too foon,
And clogg'd the midnight hour.
'Twas then, when luft's malignant fway
Had ftifled confcience' pang, and fmother'd reafon's ray,
That Mercy ftept between
Th' adult'rer, and his finful fcene;
And painted on his mental fight,
Drefs'd round in beams divinely bright,
The Saviour ftretch'd upon the tree,
In purple fweats, and dying agony:
(Such was the vifion, and the blaze the fame,
That Saul, intent on murders, faw
When Jefus, fpeaking from the radiant flame,
O'erwhelm'd his confcious foul with awe.)
Then thus a voice arrefts his ear:
" See Gard'ner, fee thy Saviour here!
" And was this wood
" Ting'd in my blood,
" And did I languifh in thefe woes for thee,
And can'ft thou plunge thefe recent wounds in me?"
O'erpowr'd with vaft furprize,
A pris'ner of the fkies
The fwooning champion falls,
And fear, that never yet his foul had fhook,
Bedews his limbs, glares wild upon his look,
And all his foul appalls:
But half the agony was unfulfill'd,
Till Mercy from her cryftal urn inftill'd
Fierce on his heart three burning drops, *
Drops that from Sinai came,
From Sinai, where th' Almighty thunderer forms
His fhafted lightnings, and his bolted ftorms,

* See Milton's Paradife loft, B. xi, Lin. 416.

And from whofe boiling tops
The wild fulphureous furge runs down in liquid flame,
    Stung with th' unfufferable fmart,
        That feſter'd at his heart,
    Gard'ner awakes, and round he throws
    His ghaſtly eyes, and fcarce he knows
Or if he lives in nature's midnight gloom,
Or, clos'd in hell's unfathomable womb,
Black o'er his head eternal horrors roll,
And the keen gnawing worm devours his inmoſt foul.

VII.

    But when his wand'ring thought had found
        Himſelf a tenant of the ground,
    Still, ſtill his confcience felt the flaming wound.
        Sudden before his profpeſt glows
        The everlaſting gulph of woes ;
    From the o'er hanging brink he ſeems to bend,
        (The bri k, that crumbled as he ſtood,
        And nodded o'er the dreadful flood,)
    And down in headlong ruin to defcend
To the broad burning waves, and pains that never end.
        He turns ; but ah ! no friendly hand,
        Nor fpark of glimm'ring hope, appears
    Amidſt the raging torment of his fears,
    But, outlaw'd from the realms of ſhining blifs,
    He thinks he feels the unextinguiſh'd fires,
    A waving waſte of blue a'ceuding fpires,
    And plunges in the bottomlefs abyfs :
    For, oh ! his fins in crouding numbers ſtand,
        And each tempts vengeance from th' Almighty hand :
But fiercer o'er the reſt ingratitude appears,
That fcorn'd the Saviour's love, and flaming horrors wears.
        But while in fad confufion tofs'd,
            And tortur'd with defpair
        He doom'd his foul for ever loſt,
            The bright ætherial Fair
            (For 'twas her kind defign
        Not to deſtroy but to refine,)
        Amidſt the darknefs and the ſtorms
        Her facred embaſſy performs ;
    For guilt difplay'd in all its frightful dyes,

And crimſon'd over with redeeming blood,
  Draws out the rolling anguiſh from his eyes,
And all his ſtubborn ſoul with low ſubmiſſion bow'd.
  'Tis done : O miracle of leve !
  Not minds below, nor minds above,
  Great God, can trace thy myſtic ways,
  And pay the equal note of praiſe.
  'Tis done : And now with outſtretch'd wings
Back to the ſkies the radiant Pow'r withdrew ;
  And, as her mounting path ſhe ſprings,
  The ſilver trump of victory ſhe blows,
  In ſtronger dyes her arch refulgent glows,
And a far ſtreaming glory tracks th' ætherial blue.

VIII

  At once abjuring all his ſins,
  Gard'ner the heav'nly life begins,
  And pleads the honours of his God
  With irreſiſtible defence
Againſt the colour'd arts of eloquence,
Though clouded with his Maker's frown, and cruſh'd be-
                     (neath his rod.
  But quickly a celeſtial ray
  Shot o'er his ſoul unclouded day,
  And balmy dews, and blooming life were giv'n,
  The early antepaſt of heav'n.
  And now what equal words ſhall paint
  How Gard'ner, freed from tyrant luſts,
  Nor longer tofs'd in paſſion's guſts,
  Felt, ſpoke, and acted all the ſaint ?
That holy name, which he prophan'd before,
Behold him now with ſuppliant knee adore ;
At morn and ev'n his warm devotions riſe,
Like clouds of incenſe, fragrant to the ſkies :
  No more the grape's nectareous juice
  Could tempt beyond a prudent uſe ;
  No wanton ſpeech defil'd his tongue ;
  No deed deſign'd his neighbour wrong :
  But the fair ſtreams of innocence,
  And unconfin'd benevolence,
O'er all his life uninterrupted ran.
And through their cryſtal mirrors ſhew'd the man.
  The num'rous characters he bore

With a diftinguifh'd praife he wore,
And fubjeĉt, foldier, hufband, parent, friend,
He blended, and ennobled to the end.
Now with feraphic tranfports fir'd,
The pinions of his zeal afpir'd,
Scarce patient till he broke the mortal fhell,
And bid this empty fcene, and dufky globe farewell.
Heav'n was his home, and to his home he bent,
And e're the rounds of fatal life were fpent,
Thither his paffions would divinely roll,
The fwift-wing'd heralds of his coming foul.
Peace at his tent would often light, and fing,
And fhed the dewy bleffings from her wing ;
And rills, devolving from the fount above,
Pour'd o'er his heart extatic life and love,

IX.

Thus Gard'ner liv'd ; till from the gloomy north
Rebellion, grafping targe and fteely arms,
Rufh'd, like a mountain boar, impetuous forth,
And fhook our realms with horrible alarms ;
Rebellion aiming at one wafteful fway
To ftrike the diadem from Brunfwick's head,
Tear liberty, and all her mounds away,
And Popery's o'erwhelming horrors fpread.
The news to Gard'ner came,
And fann'd the noble flame,
Which pure Religion, heav'n-born Liberty,
And dauntlefs Fortitude had rais'd ;
And, as the gath'ring terrors thunder'd nigh,
With a redoubled ftrength the mounting fervors blaz'd.
What, though diftemper had fubdu'd his limbs,
And age defrauded half the purple ftreams,
That bloom'd his features o'er,
When in Rebellion's ftorm before,
He, rifing in the glorious caufe
Of George's rights, and Britain's Laws,
Swept down the trait'rous files, and Prefton fwam with
(gore?
Yet his unbroken foul difdains
Age's dull load of cramps and pains ;
His youthful rage returns,
And for the battle burns :

Then, fpringing from Franciffa's tender arms,
Diffolv'd in flowing tears,
Oe'rwhelm'd with boding fears,
And only folac'd with the view
That heav'n their friendfhip would renew;
He, in th' unfhaken confidence of pray'r,
Sways the keen flame of his revenging fword
For his eternal, and his earthly Lord,
Serenely meets the dangers wild alarms,
Plants his embattled force, and waits the rufhing war.
So Michael, * bent on glorious fight,
Againft Satanic rage and might,
Came tow'ring to the field;
Unconfcious of a quiv'ring fear,
He faw the foe his dufky horrors rear,
Wave his broad flaming fword, and heave his moony fhield,

X.

Not far from where Edina lifts
Her tow'rs into the fkies,
Or where the ocean-bounding clifts
In clouded fummits rife,
Prefton extends her humble cots,
Long, long unknown to fame,
But flying routs, and purple fpots
Have ftamp'd th' eternal fhame.
Here, here, (oh could time's brazen pen
Dafh the reproach away,
Or, as the day returns again,
Might midnight choak its rays!)
Britania's troops in vain
Oppos'd the Rebel-hoft,
And fled inglorious o'er the plain,
Their courage wither'd, and their ftandards loft.
Mufe, paint the doleful fcene
With fighs and tears between;
For fighs and tears fhould rife
From ev'ry Britifh heart, and gufh from all our eyes.
Swift on the loyal van
The yelling furies ran,
Like the wild ocean that has rent

---

* Milton's Paradife Laft, B. vi. L. 225.

Its fhores, and rears along the continent ;
Or the wing'd light'nings livid glare
Darting along th' immeafur'd fields of air.
　　Confounded at the fhock,
　　The yielding fqu..drons broke :
And now, (for hell infpir'd the throng,)
　The gloomy murd rers ruth'd along ;
　　And fierce the fteely blade,
　　Its horrid circles play'd,
　　　　Till hideous cries,
　　　　Quiv'ring fighs,
　　　　Hopelefs fcreams,
　　　　Batter'd limbs,
　　　　Bloody ftreams,
And univerfal rout deform'd the ground,
Laid wafte the Britifh ftrength, and the wide champion
　　　　　　　　　　　　　　　(drown'd

　　" Come on, come on," mad Flcho cries.
And for his murders thanks the fkies,
(While the Italian from afar,
Too foft a foul to mix in war,
Enjoying all the guilt, beheld
His bloody harpies tear the field,)
　" Ply, ply the thirfty fteel,
　" Round the full vengeance wheel ;
" Each heretic muft yield his breath
" That for the Hanoverian brood
　　" Or lifts a fword,
　　" Or fpeaks a word ;
　" Come, gorge your fouls with death,
　" And drown your fteps in blood ;
" Think, think what blefsful periods roll behind,
　" Let London's mighty plunder fill your mind,
" When boundlefs wealth fhall be with boundlefs empire
　　　　　　　XI.　　　　　　　(join'd."

　　Gard'ner, with mind elate
　　Above the rage of fate,
　　His country's bulwark ftood.
'Midft broken lines of death, and rifing waves of blood,
　　His foul difdains retreat,
　　Though urg'd by foul defeat,
　Now to his fcatt'ring friends he calls,

To wheel again and charge the foe ;
Now hurls the wide deltroying balls,
Now deals the vengeful blow;
Forfaken and alone,
And torn with gafhing wounds,
He hears the treas'uous fhout, he hears the loyal groan ;
But nought the purpofe of his foul confounds :
And ftill with new delight
He tempts the midmoft fight,
Prop'd on his facred caufe, and courage of his own.
Th' embattled ranks of foot he fpies
Without a leading chief,
And like a fhooting ray, he flies
To lend his brave relief.
Here the broad weapon's forceful fway,
Swung with tempeftuous hand,
Plough'd through his flefh its furious way,
And ftretch'd him on the ftrand.
Welt'ring in gore, with fiery fiends befet,
The dying Gard'ner lies ;
No gentle hand to wipe the mortal fweat,
And clofe his fwimming eyes.
The unrelenting crew
The hero difarray'd ;
But ftruck at his majeftic view,
Their fou's were half difmay'd :
And, had not hell inftamp'd its hate,
Their ftony eye-balls o'er his fate
Had ftream'd with human woe ; for heav'nly mild
He o'er the gloomy forms the Chriftian pardon fmil'd.
But not a tear moft bathe, or garment fhield
His mangled limbs from fight,
Down-trodden in the fight :
While his fair manfion, that o'er tops the field,
The naked youth r fees, and trembles from its height.
Still the departing flame of life
Wav'd languifhing in doubtful ftrife ;
Till, fuch his fervant's faithful care,
(May heav'as diftinguifh'd goodnefs crown
The good it fs to his mafter fhown !)
The wheels flow-moving, from the fcenes of war,
To Tranent bore th' expiring chief,

In fullen founds remurm'ring to his grief.
Urania, mark the melancholy road,
with thy tears efface the fcatt'ring blood ;
Nor ftop, till on the late repofing bed
(Oh ! rather 'tis the fun'ral bier !)
You fee the hero's pallid body fpread,
   And his laſt anguiſh hear.
   Half-choak'd with clotted gore,
   He draws the hollow moan ;
Flitting his pulfe, and fix'd his eyes,
All pale and motionlefs he lies,
   And feems to breathe no more.———
  Oh ! that's the life-diffolving groan :———
Farewel, dear man ! for in that pang thy mind
Soars to its God, and leaves the clog behind.
         X I.
Gard'ner is dead !———The bloody trump of fame
   Proclaim'd the mighty death ;
In ev'ry look the pofting rumor came,
   And flew on ev'ry breath,
The widow'd partner of his life
The doleful tidings hears,
And, filent in ftupendous grief,
   Her eyes refufe their tears :
Opprefs'd beneath th' immeafurable weight,
   Her fpirit faints away,
As, fmpathetic with the hero's fate,
   It meant to quit its clay.
   The pledges of his love
   Their filial duty prove,
And each with tender hands uprears,
With hands all cover'd o'er in tears,
   Their mother's finking head ;
   And groan refounds to groan
For oh ! the beſt of hufbands gone,
   The beſt of fathers dead !
But Gard'ner's death is more than private woe ;
Wide and more wide th' increafing forrows run,
   O'er Britifh lands unlimited they go,
  And fly acrofs the feas and travel with the fun,
Religion, that from heav'n had bow'd
   To watch the fcale of fight,

When holy Gard'ner fell,
Who lov'd, and who adorn'd her caufe fo well,
Retir'd behind a crimfon cloud,
Nor could fuftain the fight.
Britania, where fhe fate
Upon the fea beat-fhore
To eye the battle's fate,
Her filver mantle tore :
Then thus, her blufhing honours wann'd,.
Her fceptre quiv'ring in her hand,
Her laurels wither'd, and her head delin'd,
Ten thoufand terrors bod:ng in her mind,
She to the deep in bitter wailing griev'd :
While her fall'n helm the trickling drops reciev'd:
   " What havock of my martial force
    " Has this fad morn beheld,
   " Torn, gafh'd, and heap'd without remorfe
    " Upon the naked field ?
   " But Gard'ner's death afflicts me moft,
   " Than whom a chief I could not boaft
   " More faithful, vigilant, and brave ;
    " And fhould acrofs his grave
  " An Hecatomb of Highland brutes be flain,
  " They could not recompenfe his injur'd ghoft,
" Nor fully quench my rage, and wipe away my ftain."

XI.

But fee, in fplendid ftate
Cherubic convoys come,
And waft the hero from his fate
To his celeftial home.
Now, now he fails along,
Encircled with their throng,
(The throng, that clap their mantling wings.
And to loud triumphs ftrike their ftrings,)
Thro' liquid feas of day
Ploughing the azure way,
Till to the ftarry tow'rs the fquadrons rife.
The ftarry tow'rs, thick fown with pearl and gold,
  Their adamantine leaves unfold;
And fhew the entrance to th' empyreal fkies :
Through them our hero mark'd his road,
And through the wheeling ranks of heav'n

An unobſtructed path was giv'n,
Till he attain'd th' eternal throne of God ;
A throne that blaz'd in uncreated beams,
And from its footſtool guſh'd unnumber'd ſtreams,
Streams, that in everlaſting currents roll,
And pour the boundlefs joy o'er all th' expanded foul.
Well haſt thou done, th' Almighty Father ſpoke ;
Well haſt thou done, th' exalted Jeſus cry'd ;
Well haſt thou done, (all heav'n the Enge took,)
The faints and angels in their fongs reply'd.
    And now a robe of ſpotlefs white,
    But where the Saviour's flowing vein
    Had bluſh'd it with a fanguine ſtain,
    Invefts him round : In various light
    (For fuch was the divine command,)
Refulgent on his brows a crown was plac'd ;
And a triumphal palm his better hand
        With golden bloſſoms grac'd.
        Nigh to the feat of blifs
        His manfion was affign'd ;
    Sorrow and fin forfook his breaſt,
    His weary foul was now at reſt,
    And life, and love, and extafies
Unbound his fecret pow'rs, and overflow'd his mind.
                XIV.
    Nor has thy life, heroic man been fpilt
    Without a wrath proportion'd to the guilt ;
        Enkindled by the cries that rofe
        From thy dear facred blood, with thofe
    That ſhriek'd for vengeance from the brave Munro's,
        Who fell a martyr'd facrifice
        To cool remorfelefs butcheries,
    Heav'n fends its angel righteouſly fevere,
    And from the foe exacts the laft arrear.
        For when the barb'rous bands,
    Thick as the fwarms that black'ned Egypt's ſtrands,
    And furious as the winter's ruſhing rains
        Impell'd by whirlwinds thro' the plains,
        Had o'er our country roll'd,
    Young William rofe. (aufpicious name,
    Sacred to liberty and fame !)
                M

And their mad rage controul'd.
Back to their hills and bogs they fled,
(For terror wing'd their nimble fpeed,)
     And howl'd for help in vain :
William purfu'd, and launch'd his vengeful ire,
(As o'er the ftubble runs the crackling fire,)
     Upon the grov'ling train :
Shudd'ring with horror and defpair
With bell'wing pain they rend the air,
Till Culloden's illuftrious moor
Groan'd with the heaps of flain, and fmoak'd with rebel-
                                                (gore.

     Then, mufe. fupprefs thy rifing fighs,
     And wipe the anguifh from thine eyes ;
Sing how Rebellion has receiv'd its doom,
How Gard'ner dwells in his eternal home,
And in each Britifh heart has rais'd a lafting tomb.

THE

CHRISTIAN WARRIOR

ANIMATED and *CROWNED:*

A SERMON

Occafioned by the HEROIC DEATH of the Honourable

Col. JAMES GARDINER,

Who was flain in the Battle at PRESTON-PANS, *September* 21, 1745.

Preached at NORTHAMPTON, October 13.

By P. DODDRIDGE, D. D.

——————— *Ille* Timorum
Maximus *haud urget Lethi Metus :*———
———*Ignavum* REDITURÆ *parcere Vitæ.*

LUCAN.

PHILADELPHIA:

PRINTED AND SOLD BY STEWART & COCHRAN,
Nº. 34, SOUTH SECOND-STREET.

M, DCC, XCV.

TO THE

RIGHT HONOURABLE THE

Lady *FRANCES GARDINER.*

MADAM,

THE intimate knowledge I had of Colonel Gardiner's private as well as public character, and of that indeared friendſhip which ſo long ſubſiſted between him and your ladyſhip, makes me more ſenſible than moſt others can be, both of the inexpreſſible loſs you have ſuſtained, and of the exquiſite ſenſe you have of it. I might, in ſome degree, argue what you felt from the agony with which my own heart was torn by that ever to be lamented ſtroke, which deprived the nation, and the church, of ſo great an ornament and bleſſing: And indeed, madam, I was ſo ſenſible of your calamity, as to be ready in my firſt thoughts to congratulate you, when I heard the report which at firſt prevailed, that you died under the ſhock. Yet cooler reflections, teaches me, on many accounts, to rejoice that your ladyſhip has ſurvived that deareſt part of yourſelf; though after having been ſo lovely and pleaſant in your lives, it would have been matter of perſonal rejoicing, in death not to have been divided. The numerous and promiſing offspring with which God hath bleſſed your marriage, had evidently the higheſt intereſt in the continued life of ſo pious and affectionate a mother: And I hope, and aſſuredly believe, there was a more important, and to you a much dearer intereſt concerned, as God may be, and is ſignally honoured, by the manner in which you bear this heavieſt and moſt terrible ſtroke of his paternal rod.

God had been pleaſed, madam, to make you both eminent for a variety of graces; and he has proportionably diſtinguiſhed you both in the opportunity he has given you of

M 2

exercifing thofe, which fuit the moſt painful ſcenes, that can attend a pious and an honourable life. But when I conſider, what it is, to have loſt ſuch a man, at ſuch time, and in ſuch circumſtances, I muſt needs declare, that brave and heroic as the death of the colonel was, your ladyſhip's part is beyond all comparifon the hardeſt. Yet even here has the grace of Chriſt been fufficient for you; and I join with your ladyſhip in adoring the power and faithfulnefs of him, who has here ſo remarkably ſhewn, that he forgets not his promiſe to all his people of a ſtrength proportionable to their days; that they may be enabled to glorify him in the hotteſt furnace, into which it is poffible they ſhould be caſt.

To hear, (as I have heard from ſeveral perſons of diſtinguiſhed character, who have lately had the happinefs of being near your ladyſhip,) of that meek refignation to the divine will, of that calm patience, of that chriſtian courage, with which, in ſo weak a ſtate of health and ſpirits, you have fupported under this awful providence, has given me great pleafure but no furprize. So near a relation to ſo brave a man might have taught ſome degree of fortitude, to a ſoul lefs fufceptible of it than your ladyſhip's. Nor is there any doubt, but that the prayers he has ſo long been laying up in ſtore for you, eſpecially ſince the decay of his conſtitution gave him reafon to expect a ſpeedy remove, will affuredly at ſuch a feafon come into remembrance before God. And above all, the fublime principles of the chriſtian religion, ſo deeply imbibed into your own heart as well as his, will not fail to exert their energy on ſuch an occafion. Thefe, madam, will teach you to view the hand of a wife, a righteous, and a gracious God in this event; and will ſhew you, that a friendſhip founded on ſuch a bafis, ſo very indearing, and ſo clofely cemented, as that which has been here for many years a blefſing to you both, can know only a very ſhort interruption, and will ſoon grow up into a union infinitely nobler and more delightful, which never ſhall be liable to any feparation.

In the mean time, madam, it may comfort us not a little under the fenfe of our prefent lofs, to think what religious improvement we may gain by it, if we are not wauting to ourfelves: And happy ſhall we be indeed, if we ſo hear the rod, as to receive the inſtructions it ſo naturally fuggeſts and inforces. Perfons of any ferious reflection will learn from this awful event, how little we can judge of the divine favour by the vifible difpenfations of providence here : They will learn, (and it may be of great importance to confider it, juft in fuch a crifis as this,) that no diftinguifhed degree of piety can fecure the very beft of men from the fword of a common enemy : And they will fee (written, alas, in characters of the moft precious blood, that war ever fpilt in our ifland,) the vanity of the fureft protectors and comforters which mortality can afford, at a time when they are moft needed.

Thefe are general inftructions, which I hope thoufands will receive, on this univerfally lamented occafion : But to you, madam, and to me, and to all that were honoured with the moft intimate friendfhip of this chriftian hero, his death has a peculiar voice. Whilft it leads us back into fo many paft fcenes of delight, in the remembrance of which we now pour out our fouls within us, it calls aloud, amidft all this tender diftrefs, for a tribute of humble thankfulnefs to God, that ever we enjoyed fuch a friend, and efpecially in fuch an intimacy of mutual affection ; and that we had an opportunity of obferving, in fo many inftances, the fecret receffes of a heart, which God had enriched, adorned, and ennobled with fo much of his own image, and fuch abundant communications of his grace : It calls for our redoubled diligence and refolution, in imitating that bright affemblage of virtues, which fhone fo refplendent in our illuftrious friend : And furely it muft, by a kind of irrefiftible influence mortify our affections to this impoverifhed world ; and muft caufe nature to concur with grace, in raifing our hearts upwards to that glorious world where he dwells triumphant and immortal, and waits our arrival with an ardor of pure and elevated love, which it was impoffible for death to quench.

Next to thefe views, nothing can give your ladyfhip greater fatisfaction, than to reflect, how happy you made the amiable confort you have loft, in that intimate relation you fo long bore to each other ; in which, I well know, that growing years ripened and increafed your mutual efteem and friendfhip. Nor will your generous heart be infenfible of that pleafure, which may arife from reflecting, that the manner of his death (tho' in itfelf fo terrible, that we dare not truft imagination with the particular review,) was to him, in thofe circumftances, moft glorious to religion, highly ornamental, and to his country (great as its lofs is,) on various accounts beneficial. For very far be it from us to think, that Colonel Gardiner, tho' fallen by the weapons of rebellion and treafon, has fought and died in vain. I truft in God, that fo heroic a behaviour will infpire our warriors with augmented courage, now they are called to exert it in a caufe, the moft noble and important that can ever be in queftion, the caufe of our laws, our liberty and religion. I truft, that all who keep up a correfpondence with heaven by prayer, will renew their interceffion for this bleeding land with increafing fervour, now we have loft one who ftood in the breach with fuch unwearied importunity. And I am well affured, that of the multitudes who lay up his memory in their inmoft hearts with veneration and love, not a few will be often joining their moft affectionate prayers to God, for your ladyfhip, and the dear rifing branches of your family, with thofe which you may, in confequence of a thoufand obligations, always expect from

M A D A M ,

Your ladyfhip's moft faithful

and obedient humble fervant,

P. DODDRIDGE.

Northampton.
Nov. 27, 1745.

Rev. ii. 10. latter Part.

—— *Be thou faithful unto Death, and I will give thee a Crown of Life.*

IT is a glory peculiar to the Christian religion, that it is capable of yielding joy and triumph to the mind amidst calamities, in which the strength of nature, and of a philosophy that has no higher a support, can hardly give it serenity, or even patience. Those boasted aids are but like a candle in some tempestuous night, which how artificially soever it may be fenced in, is often extinguished amidst the storm, in which it should guide and chear the traveller, or the mariner, whom it leaves on a sudden, in darkness, horror, and fear : while the consolation of the gospel, like the sun, makes a sure day even when behind the thickest cloud, and soon emerges from it with an accession of more sensible lustre.

The observation is verified in these words considered in connection with that awful providence, which has this day determined my thoughts to fix upon them, as the subject of my discourse ; the fall of that truly great and good man, Col. Gardiner : the endearing tenderness of whose friendship would have rendered his death an unspeakable calamity to me, had his character been only of the common standard ; as on the other hand, the exalted excellency of his character makes his death to be lamented by thousands, who were not happy in any peculiar intimacy or personal acquaintance with him.

While we mourn the brave warrior, the exemplary Christian, and the affectionate friend ; left to ourselves and our country, to the church and the world, at a time when we most needed all the defence of his bravery, all the edification of his example, all the comfort of his converse : struck with the various and aggravated sorrow of so sudden, and so terrible a blow, methinks there is but one voice that can chear us, which is this of the great Captain of our salvation, so lately addressing him, and still addressing us, in these comprehensive and animated words ; " Be thou faithful unto death, and I will give thee a crown of life."

With regard to the connection of them, it may be sufficient to observe, that our Lord in all these seven epistles to the Asiatic churches represents the Christian life as a warfare, and the blessings of the future state as rewards to be bestowed on conquerors. "To him that overcometh, will I give" such and such royal donatives. Pursuing the same allegory, he warns the church of Smyrna of an approaching combat, which should be attended with some severe circumstances. Some of them were to become captives; "the devil shall cast some of you into prison:" and though the power of the enemy was to be limited, in its extent as well as its duration, to the tribulation of ten days, it seems to be implied, that while many were harrassed and distressed during that time, some of them should before the close of it be called to resist unto blood. But their great Leader furnishes them with suitable armour, and proportionable courage, by this gracious assurance, which it is our present business farther to contemplate: "Be thou faithful unto death, and I will give thee a crown of life."

In which words you naturally observe a charge,—and a promise by which it is inforced—I shall briefly illustrate each, and then conclude with some reflections upon the whole.

FIRST. I am to open the charge here given: "Be thou faithful unto death"

Concerning which I would observe, that though it is immediately addressed to the church at Smyrna, yet the nature of the thing and numberless passages of the divine word concur to prove, that it is common in its obligation, to all Christians, and indeed to all men.

I shall not be large in explaining the nature of faithfulness in general; concerning which I might shew you, that the word here rendered faithful has sometimes a relation to the testimony which God has given us, and sometimes to some trust that he has reposed in us. In the former sense, it is properly rendered believing, and opposed to infidelity: "Be not faithless, but believing."* In the latter, it is opposed to injustice: "He that is faithful in that which is least, is faithful also in much;" whereas "he that is unjust in the least, is unjust also in much"† And it is in reference to this sense of it, that our Lord represents himself, as saying to the man who had improved his talents aright, "Well

---

* John xx. 27.   † Luke xvi 10.

one, good and faithful fervant."* Our deceafed friend was
a remarkably faithful in both thefe fenfes; fo ready to ad-
nit, and fo zealous to defend " the faith once delivered to
he faints;" and fo active in improving thofe various talents,
with which, in mercy to many others as well as to himfelf,
God had entrufted him ; that it was very natural to touch
pon thefe fignifications of the word, though it has here a
nore particular view to another virtue, for which he was fo
illuftrioufly confpicuous; I mean, the courageous fidelity of
foldier in his warfare.

In this fenfe of the word, it is oppofed to treachery or
owardice, defertion or difobedience to military orders. And
hus it is ufed elfewhere in the fame book of the Revelation,
when fpeaking of thofe who war under the banner of the
Lamb, the King of kings, and Lord of lords, the infpired
writer tells us, " they are called, and chofen, and faithful,"†
felect body of brave and valiant foldiers.

This hint will alfo fix the eafieft and plaineft fenfe in
which the perfons, to whom the text is addreffed, are required to be faithful unto death : which, though it does indeed
ii general imply, a patient continuance in well-doing,‖ in
whatever fcenes of life divine Providence may place us ; yet
oes efpecially refer to martial bravery, and exprefs a readi-
efs to face death in its moft terrible forms, when our great
General fhall lead us on to it. You well know this to be an
indifpenfable condition of our being acknowledged by him
a the day of his final triumph : and of this he warned thofe
hat gathered around him, when he was firft raifing his ar-
ny. under the greateft difadvantages in outward appearance;
xprefsly and plainly telling them, that they muft be content
a follow him to martyrdom, to follow him to crucifixion,
when they receive the word of command to do it ; or that
il their profeffion of regard to him would be in vain. " If
any man." fays he, " will come after me, let him deny him-
lf and take up his crofs and follow me :"§ For " he that
iveth his own life more than me, is not worthy of me ;"¶
e does not deferve the honour of bearing my name, and
alling for one of my foldiers ; indeed he cannot on any
:rms be my difciple.**

This therefore is in effect the language of our Lord, when

* Mat. xxv. 23.   † Rev. xvii. 14.   ‖ Rom. ii. 7.
§ Mark viii. 34.   ¶ Mat. x. 37, 39.   ** Luke xiv. 26.

he fays, " Be thou faithful unto death :" It
faid, " Remember, all you of Smyrna, or of
" and country, that call yourfelves Chriftia
" all generations, that you were by baptifn
" my banners : Remember, that you have a
" and fubfcribed your engagement to me,
" ment you have fince attended ;" (as inc
known, the word facrament originally fign
oath, which foldiers took as a pledge of fidel
neral :) " Remember therefore, that you ar
" nue with me, and to march forward unde
" whatever hardfhips and fatigues may lie in
" remember, that if I lead you on to the i
" combat, you muft cheerfully obey the wor
" and charge boldly, though you fhould it
" whether by the fword, or by fire. Should
" I am myfelf your enemy ; and the weapor
" would juftly be levelled at your own traitor
" if you bravely follow me, I know how to
" ple amends, even though you fall in the ad
" human power and gratitude can reach you, i
" prerogative to engage, that to thofe who a
" unto death, I will give a crown of life." W

SECONDLY, To confider the Promife,
   Charge is enforced : ' I will give thee a
   And here I might obferve,—a Crown of
rious reward propofed,—and it is to be rec
hand of Chrift.

   1. A Crown of Life is the reward propo
   are fure in this connection implies, both
   felicity, here, though rarely connected
   There is, no doubt, an allufion in thefe wc
cient, and I think very prudent cuftom, of
bravery of foldiers by honorary rewards, and
crowns, fometimes of laurel, and fometimes,
filver or gold ; which they were permitted to
occafions, and in confequence of receiving w
fometimes intitled to fome peculiar immunitic
Lord Jefus Chrift, confcious of his own div
prerogative, fpeaks with a dignity and elevat
earthly prince or commander could ever affu
a crown of life, and that (as was obferved I

thofe who fhould fall in the battle : A crown of life in the higheft fenfe ; not only one, which fhould ever be frefh and fair, but which fhould give immortality to the happy brow it adorned ; and be for ever worn, not only as the monument of bravery and victory, but as the enfign of royalty too : A crown connected with a kingdom, and with what no other kingdom can give, perpetual life to enjoy it ; perpetual youth and vigour to relifh all its delights. And this is agreeable to the language of other fcriptures, where we read of " the crown of life, which the Lord hath promifed to them that love him ;* a crown of righteoufnefs, which the Lord the righteous Judge fhall give ;† a crown of glory, which fadeth not away."§ We may alfo obferve,

2. That it is faid to be given by Chrift.

This fome pious commentators have explained, as intimating, that it is the gift of the Redeemer's free and unmerited grace, and not a retribution due to the merit of him that receiveth it. And this is an undoubted truth, which it is of the higheft importance to acknowledge and confider. The proper wages of fin, is death ; but eternal life is (in oppofition to wages) " the gift of God through Jefus Chrift our Lord."‖ We fhould humbly own it every day, that there is no proportion between the value of our fervices, and the crown which we expect to receive : fhould own, that it is mercy that pardons our fins, and grace that accepts our fervices ; much more, that crowns them. Grace, grace, fhall (as it were) be engraven upon that crown, in characters large and indelible. Nor will that infcription diminifh its luftre, or impair the pleafure with which we fhall receive it. I could not forbear mentioning this thought, as a truth of the utmoft importance, which ftands on the firmeft bafis of very many exprefs fcriptures ; a truth, of which perhaps no man living had ever a deeper fenfe, than our deceafed friend. But I mention it thus obliquely, becaufe it may be doubted whether we can juftly argue it from hence ; fince the word give is fometimes ufed for rendering a retribution juftly due, and that in inftances where grace and favour have, in propriety of fpeech, no concern at all.¶

N

* Jam. i. 12. † 2 Tim. iv. 8. § 1 Pet. v. 4. ‖ Rom. vi. 23.
¶ Compare Mat. xx. 8. Give the labourers their hire. Col. iv.
1. Mafters, give unto your fervants that which is juft and equal.

But it is certain, that this expression, "I will give thee a crown of life," is intended to lead our thoughts to this important circumstance; that this crown is to be received from the hand of Christ himself. And the apostle Paul evidently refers to the same circumstance, in terms which shew how much he entered into the spirit of the thought, when he says, "The Lord the righteous Judge shall give it me:"* He himself, the great Judge of the contest, whose eye witnesses the whole course of it, whose decision cannot err, and from whose sentence there is no appeal: Alluding to the judge who presided in the Grecian games, who was always a person of rank and eminence, and himself reached forth the reward to him who overcame in them.

So that on the whole, when our Lord Jesus Christ says, " Be thou faithful unto death, and I will give thee a crown of life," methinks our devout meditations may expatiate upon the words in some such paraphrase as this. It is as if he had said to you, and to me, and to all his people, " Oh my " faithful soldiers. fear not death in its most terrible array, " for you are immortal. Fear not them that can kill the bo- " dy ;"† You have a nobler part, which they cannot reach; " and I will undertake not only for its rescue, but its hap- " piness. I will answer for it, on the honour of my royal " word, that it shall live in a state of noble enlargement. of " triumphant joy. Think on me: I am he that liveth, " though I was dead ; and behold I am alive for evermore:§ " And because I live, you shall live also ;‖ shall exist in a " state, that deserves the great and honourable name of Life ; " so that earth in all its lustre and pleasure, when compared " with it, is but as a scene of death, or at best as an amusing " dream when one awaketh."¶

We may also consider him, as pursuing this animating address, and saying, " My brave companions in tribulation " and patience, you shall not only live, but reign. Think " not, thou good soldier, who art now fighting under my " banner, that thy general will wear his honours alone. If " I have my crown, if I have my triumph, be assured that " thou also shalt have thine. Thou mayest indeed seem to " perish in the combat, and thy friends may mourn, and " thine enemies insult, as if thou wert utterly cut off. But

* 2 Tim. iv. 8. † Mat. x. 28. § Rev. i. 18.
‖ John xiv. 19. ¶ Psalm lxxiii. 20.

" behold, true victory fpreads over thee her golden wing,
" and holds out, not a garland of fading flowers or leaves,
" but a crown that fhall keep its luftre, when all the coftlieft
" gems on earth are melted in the general burning; yea,
" when the luminaries of heaven are extinguifhed, and the
" fun and ftars fade away in their orbs."

" Nor will I," does he feem to fay, " fend thee this crown
" by fome inferior hand ; not even by the nobleft angel,
" that waits on the throne I have now afcended. Thou
" fhalt receive it from mine own hand;" (from that hand,
which would make the leaft gift valuable : What a dignity
then will it add to the greateft !) " Nor will I myfelf con-
" fer his reward in private ; it fhall be given with the moft
" magnificent folemnity. Thou fhalt be brought to me be-
" fore the affembled world ; thy name fhall be called over ;
" thou fhalt appear, and I will own thee, and crown thee,
" in public view. Thy friends fhall fee it with raptures of
" joy, and congratulate an honour in which they fhall alfo
" fhare. Thine enemies fhall fee it with envy and with
" rage, to increafe their confufion and mifery : They fhall
" fee, that while by their malicious affaults they were en-
" deavouring to deftroy thee, they were only eftablifhing
" thy throne, and brightening the luftre, which fhall for
" ever adorn thy brow ; while theirs is blafted with the
" thunder of refiftlefs wrath, and deep engraven with the in-
" delible marks of vengeance. This crown fhalt thou for
" ever wear, as the perpetual token of my efteem and af-
" fection. Nor fhall it be merely a fhining ornament : A
" rich revenue, a glorious authority, goes along with it.
" Thou fhalt reign for ever and ever;* and be a king, as
" well as a prieft, unto God."†

They who enter by a lively faith into the import of thefe
glorious words, will (I doubt not) pardon my having expati-
ated fo largely upon them. " We have believed, and therefore have we fpoken :"§ And I queftion not, but that many
of you have in the courfe of this reprefentation prevented me
in fome of the reflections, which naturally arife from fuch a
fubject. Yet it may not be improper to affift your devout
meditations upon them,

(1.) What reafon have we to adore the grace of our bleffed
Redeemer, which prepares and beftows fuch rewards as thefe!

* Rev. xxii. 5.   † Rev. i. 6.   § 2 Cor. iv. 13.

While we hear him saying, " Be thou faithful unto death,
and I will give thee a crown of life ;" methinks it is but natural for each of our hearts to answer, " Lord, dost thou
" speak of giving a crown, a crown of life and glory to me !
" Too great, too great, might the favour seem, if I, who
" have so often lifted up my rebellious hand against thy
" throne, might be allowed to lay down this guilty head
" in the dust, and lose the memory of my treasons, and the
" sense of my punishment together, in everlasting forget-
" fulness. And is such a crown prepared, and wilt thou
" my injured sovereign, who mightest so justly arm thyself
" with vengeance against me, bestow this crown with thine
" own hand; with all these other circumstances of dignity, so
" as even to make my triumphs thine own !——What is
" my strictest fidelity to thee ? though I do indeed (as I hum-
" bly desire that I may,) continue faithful unto death, I am
" yet but an unprofitable servant ; I have done no more
" than my duty.§ I have pursued thy work, in thy strength;
" and, in consequence of that love which thou hast put in-
" to my heart, it hath been its own reward : and dost thou
" thus crown one favour with another !——Blessed Jesus,
" I would with all humility lay that crown at thy feet, ac-
" knowledging before thee, and the whole world, (as I
" shall at length do in a more expressive form,) that it is
" not only the gift of thy love, but the purchase of thy blood.
" Never, never had I beheld it, otherwise than at an un-
" approachable distance, as an aggravation of my misery
" and despair, hadst not thou worn another crown, a crown
" of infamy and of thorns. The gems which must for e-
" ver adorn my temples, were formed from those precious
" drops, that once trickled down thine ; and all the splen-
" dor of my robes of triumph is owing to their being wash-
" ed in the blood of the Lamb.'‖ With what pleasing wonder may we pursue the thought ! And while it employs our
mind,

(2.) How justly may this awaken a generous ambition
to secure this crown to ourselves !

Dearly as it was purchased by our blessed Redeemer, it is
most freely offered to us, to the youngest, to the meanest,
to the most unworthy. It is not prepared, merely for those
that have worn an earthly diadem or coronet: (Would to

§ Luke xvii. 10.   ‖ Rev. vii. 14.

God, it were not defpifed by moft of them, as a thing lefs worthy of their thoughts, than the moft trifling amufement, by which they unbend their minds from the weighty cares attending their ftation!) But it is prepared for you, and for you; even for every one, who thinks it worth purfuing, and accepting, upon the terms of the gofpel covenant; for every one, who believing in Chrift, and loving him, is humbly determined through his grace to be faithful unto death.——And fhall this glorious propofal be made to you in vain? Were it an earthly crown that could lawfully be obtained, are there not many of us, notwithstanding all its weight of anxieties, and all the piercing thorns with which we might know it to be lined, that would be ready eagerly to feize it, and perhaps to contend and quarrel with each other for it? But here is no foundation for contention. Here is a crown for each; and fuch a crown, that all the royal ornaments of all the princes upon earth, when compared with it, are lighter than a feather, and viler than duft. And fhall we negleĉt it? Shall we refufe it, from fuch a hand too, as that by which it is offered? Shall we fo judge ourfelves unworthy of eternal life,* as thereby indeed to make ourfelves worthy of eternal death? For there is no other alternative.——But bleffd be God, it is not univerfally neglected. There are (I doubt not) among you many who purfue it, many who fhall affuredly obtain it For their fakes let us reflect,

(3) How courageoufly may the heads which are to wear fuch a crown, be lifted up to face all the trials of life and death!

Thofe trials may be various, and perhaps extreme; but if borne aright, far from depriving us of this crown, they will only ferve to increafe its luftre. It is the apoftle Paul's exprefs affertion; and he fpeaks as tranfported with the thought: "For this caufe we faint not, but though the outward man perifh, yet the inward man is renewed day by day: for our light affliction which is but for a moment, worketh for us a far more exceeding and eternal weight of glory, while we look not at the things which are feen, but at the things which are not feen; for the things which are feen are temporal, but the things which are not feen are eternal."† Surely with this fupport, we may not only live, but

* Aĉts xiii. 46.　　　† 2 Cor. iv. 16, 17, 18.

triumph, in poverty, in reproach, in weaknefs, in pain: And with this we may die, not only ferenely, but joyfully. Oh my friends, where are our hearts? Where is our faith? Nay, I will add, where is our reafon? Why are not our eyes, our defires, and our hopes, more frequently directed upward? Surely one ray from that refplendent diadem might be fufficient to confound all the falfe charms of thefe tranfitory vanities, wh ch indeed owe all their luftre to the darknefs in which they are placed. Surely when our fpirits are overwhelmed within us one glance of it might be fufficient to animate and elevate, and might teach us to fay, in the midft of dangers, forrows, and death, "In all thefe things we are more than conquerers, through him that loved us."* Thus have fome triumphed in the laft extremities of nature; and both the fubject, and the occafion alfo, loudly calls us to reflect,

(4.) What reafon we have to congratulate thofe happy fouls, that have already received the crown of life!

When we are weeping over the cold, yea the bleeding remains of fuch, furely it is for ourfelves, and not for them, that the ftream flows. The thought of their condition, far from moving our compaffion, may rather infpire us with joy, and with praife. Look not on their pale countenance, nor on the wide and deep wounds, through which perhaps the foul rufhed out to feize the great prize of i*s faith and hope; though even thofe wounds appear beautiful, when earned by diftinguifhed virtue, by piety to their country, and their God. Look not on the eyes clofed in death, or the once honoured and beloved head, now covered with the duft of the grave: But view, by an internal believing eye, that different form which the exalted triumphant fpirit already wears the earneft of a yet brighter glory. Their great leader, whofe care of them we are fondly ready to fufpect, or fecretly to complain of as deficient in fuch circumftances as thefe, points, (as it were) to the white robes, and the flourifhing palms, which he has given them; and calls for our regard to the crowns of life which he has fet on their heads, and to the fongs of joy and praife to which he has formed their exulting tongues. And do we fully and difhonour their triumphs with our tears? Do we think fo meanly of heaven, and of them, as to wifh them with us a-

*.Rom. viii. 37.

gain; that they might eat and drink at our tables; that they might talk with us in our low language; that they might travel with us from stage to stage in this wilderness; and take their share with us in those vanities of life, of which we ourselves are so often weary, that there is hardly a week, or a day, in which we are not lifting up our eyes, and saying with a deep inward groan, " Oh that we had wings like a dove! Then would we flee away, and be at rest.*"

Surely with relation to these faithful soldiers of Jesus Christ, who have already fallen, it is matter of no small joy to reflect, that their warfare is accomplished;† that they have at length passed through every scene in which their fidelity could be indangered; so that now, they are inviolably secure. How much more then should we rejoice, that they are entered, not only into the rest, but into the joy of their Lord; that they conquered, even when they fell, and are now reaping the fruits, the celestial and immortal fruits, of that last great victory?

A sense of honour often taught the heathens, when attending those friends to the funeral pile who had died honourably in their country's cause, to use some ceremonies expressive of their joy for their glory; though that glory was an empty name, and all the reward of it a wreath of laurel, which was soon to crackle in the flame, and vanish into smoak. And shall not the joy and glory of the living spirit affect us, much more than they could be affected with the honours paid to the mangled corpse?

Let us then think with reverence, and with joy, on the pious dead; and especially on those, whom God honoured with any special opportunities of approving their fidelity in life, or in death: And if we mourn, (as who in some circumstances, can forbear it?) Let it be as christians, with that mixture of high congratulation, with that erect countenance, and that undaunted heart, which becomes those that see by faith their exaltation and felicity; and burning with a strong and sacred eagerness to join their triumphant company, let us be ready to share in the most painful of their trials, that we may also share in their glories.

And surely, if I have ever known a life, and a death, capable of inspiring us with these sentiments in their sublimest elevations, it was the life and the death of that illus-

* Psal. lv. 6.   † Isai xl. 2.

trious chriftian hero, Colonel Gardiner; whofe character
was too well known to many of you, by fome months
refidence here, to need your being informed of it from me;
and whofe hiftory was too remarkable, to be confined within thofe few remaining moments, which muft be allotted to
the finifhing of this difcourfe. Yet there was fomething fo
uncommon in both, that I think it of high importance to the
honor of the gofpel and grace of Chrift, that they fhould be
delivered down to pofterity, in a diftinct and particular view.
And therefore, as the Providence of God, in concurrence
with that moft intimate and familiar friendfhip with which
this great and good man was pleafed to honor me, gives me
an opportunity of fpeaking of many important things, efpecially relating to his religious experiences, with greater exactnefs and certainty than moft others might be capable of
doing; and as he gave me his full permiffion, in cafe I fhould
have the afliction to furvive him, to declare freely whatever I knew of him, which I might apprehend conducive to
the glory of God, and the advancement of religion: I purpofe publifhing, in a diftinct tract, fome remarkable paffages of his life, illuftrated by extracts from his own letters,
which fpeak in the moft forcible manner the genuine fentiments of his heart. But as I promife myfelf confiderable
afliftance in this work, from fome valuable perfons in the
northern part of our ifland, and poffibly from fome of his
own papers, to which our prefent confufions forbid my accefs, I muft delay the execution of this defign at leaft for a
few months; and muft likewife take heed, that I do not too
much anticipate what I may then offer to the public view,
by what it might otherwife be very proper to mention now.

Let it therefore fuffice for the prefent to remind you, that
Colonel Gardiner was one of the moft illuftrious inftances
of the energy, and indeed I muft alfo add, of the fovereignty
of divine grace, which I have heard or read of in modern
hiftory. He was, in the moft amazing and miraculous manner, without any divine ordinance, without any religious
opportunity, or peculiar advantage, deliverance, or affliction,
reclaimed on a fudden, in the vigour of life and health, from
the moft licencious and abandoned fenfuality, not only to a
fteady courfe of regularity and virtue, but to high devotion,
and ftrict though unaffected fanctity of manners: A courfe,
(in which he perfifted for more than twenty-fix years, that

is, to the clofe of life,) fo remarkably eminent for piety towards God, diffufive humanity and Chriftian charity, lively
faith, deep humility, ftrict temperance, active diligence in
improving time, meek refignation to the will of God, fteady
patience in enduring afflictions, unaffected contempt of fecu-
lar intereft, and refolute and couragious zeal in maintaining
truth, as well as in reproving and (where his authority might
take place) reftraining vice and wickednefs of every kind ;
that I muft deliberately declare, that when I confider all thefe
particulars together, it is hard to fay where, but in the book
of God, he found his example, or where he has left his e-
qual. Every one of thefe articles, with many more, I hope,
(if God fpare my life) to have an opportunity of illuftrating,
in fuch a manner as to fhew, that he was a living demon-
ftration of the energy and excellency of the Chriftian religion ; nor can I imagine how I can ferve its interefts better, than by recording what I have feen and known upon
this head, known to my own edification, as well as my joy.

But, Oh, how fhall I lead back your thoughts, and my
own, to what we once enjoyed in him, without too deep and
tender a fenfe of what we have loft ! To have poured out his
foul in blood ; to have fallen by the favage and rebellious
hands of his own countrymen, at the wall of his own houfe;
deferted by thofe, who were under the higheft obligations
that can be imagined to have defended his life with their
own ; and above all, to have feen with his dying eyes the e-
nemies of our religion and liberties triumphant, and to have
heard in his lateft moments the horrid noife of their infulting
fhouts ;——is a fcene, in the view of which we are almoft
tempted to fay, Where were the fhields of angels ? Where
the eye of Providence ? Where the remembrance of thofe
numberlefs prayers, which had been offered to God for the
prefervation of fuch a man, at fuch a time as this ?——But
let faith affure us, that he was never more dear and precious in the eye of his divine leader, than in thefe dreadful
moments, when if fenfe were to judge, he might feem moft
neglected. That is of all others the happieft death, which
may moft fenfibly approve our fidelity to God, and our zeal
for his glory. To ftand fingly in the combat with the
fierceft enemies, in the caufe of religion and liberty, when
the whole regiment he commanded fled ; to throw himfelf
with fo noble an ardor to defend thofe on foot, whom the

whole body which he headed were appointed to support,
when he saw that the fall of the nearest commander exposed
those brave men to the extremity of danger ; were circumstances that evidently shewed, how much he held honour
and duty dearer than life. He could not but be conscious of
the distinguished profession he had made, under a religious
character ; he could not but be sensible, how much our army, in circumstances like these, needs all that the most generous examples can do, to animate its officers and its soldiers : And therefore he seems deliberately to have judged,
that although when his men would hear no voice but that of
their fears, he might have retreated without infamy, it was
better he should die in so glorious a cause, than have it
thought that his regard to religion and liberty was but a
mere profession, that was not strong enough to make him
faithful unto death. He had long felt the force of it ; and
had too high a value for his king and country, to think of
deserting the trust committed to him ; too great a love for
the protestant religion, to think of exchanging it for the
errors of popery ; and rather than give way to a rebellious
crew, by whose success an inlet would be opened to the cruel
ravages of arbitrary power, and to the bloody and relentless
rage of popish superstition, he loved not his life unto the
death*. And in this view his death was martyrdom, and
has, I doubt not, received the applauses and rewards of it :
For what is martyrdom, but voluntarily to meet death, for
the honour of God, and the testimony of a good conscience?
——And if it be indeed true, as it is reported on very
considerable authority, that before he expired he had an interview with the leader of the opposite party, and declared
in his presence " the full assurance he had of an immortal
" crown, which he was going to receive," it is a circumstance worthy of being had in everlasting remembrance :
As in that case, providence may seem wonderfully to have
united two seemingly inconsistent circumstances, in the
manner of his dying ; the alternative of either of which he
has spoken of in my hearing, as what with humble submis-
sion to the great Lord of life he could most earnestly wish :
" That if he were not called directly to die for the truth,"
which he rightly judged the most glorious and happy lot of
mortality, " he might either fall in the field of battle,

* Rev. xii. 11.

" fighting in defence of the religion and liberties of his
" country ; or might have an opportunity of expreffing his
" hopes and joys, as a chriftian, to the honour of his Lord,
" and the edification of thofe about him, in his departing
" moments ; and fo might go off this earthly ftage,' as in
the letter that relates his death, it is exprefsly faid that he
did, " triumphing in the affurance of a bleffed immortality."

How difficult it muft be in our prefent circumftances, to
gain certain and exact information, you will eafily perceive :
But enough is known, and more than enough, to fhew how
juftly the high confolations of that glorious fubject which
we have been contemplating, may be applied to the prefent
folemn occafion. From what is certain with relation to
him, we may prefume to fay, that after he had adorned
the gofpel by fo honorable a life, in fuch a confpicuous ftation, God feems to have condefcended, as with his own
hand, to raife him an illuftrious theatre, on which he might
die a venerable and amiable fpectacle to the world. and to
angels, and to men* ; ballancing to his native land by fuch
an exit, the lofs of what future fervices it could have expected, from a conftitution fo much broken as his was, by
the fatigues of his campaign in Flanders, where he contracted an illnefs, from which he never recovered.

On the whole therefore, whatever caufe we have, (as indeed we have great caufe,) to fympathize with his wounded
family, and with his wounded country ; and how decent foever it may be, like David, to take up our lamentation
over the mighty fallen, and the brighteft weapons of our
war perifhed† ; (and oh, how naturally might fome of us
adopt the preceding words too!) Yet after all, let us endeavour to fummon up a fpirit, like that with which he
bore the lofs of friends, eminent for their goodnefs and
ufefulnefs. And while we glorify God in him ‡, as on fo
many accounts we have reafon to do, let us be animated by
fuch an example to a refolution of continuing like him,
ftedfaft in our duty, amidft defertion and danger, and all
the terrors that can befet us around. As he, having been
fo eminently faithful unto death, has undoubtedly received
a crown of life, which fhines with diftinguifhed luftre,
among thofe who are come out of much tribulation|| ; let us
be couragious followers of him, and of all the glorious com-

1 Cor. iv. 9. † 2 Sam. i. 27. ‡ Gal. i. 24. || Rev. vii. 14.

pany of thofe, who through faith and patience inherit the pro-
mifes¶. Then may we be able to enter into the comfort and
fpirit of them all, and of this promife in particular; and fhall
not be difcouraged, though we are called to endure a great fight
of afflictions§, or even to facrifice our lives, like him, in defence of our religion and liberties: Since in this caufe we know,
if we fhould fall like him, even to die is gain‖; and while his
memory is bleffed†, and his name had in honour, we are affured
upon the beft authority, that having fought the good fight with fo
heroic a fortitude, and finifhed his courfe with fo fteady a tenor, and kept the faith with fo unfhaken a refolution, there is
laid up for him a crown of brighter glory than he has yet received, which the Lord the righteous judge will give unto him in
that great expected day; and not unto him only, but unto all
them that love his appearance. 2 Tim. iv. 7, 8. Amen!

¶ Heb. vi. 12.   § Heb. x. 32.   ‖ Phil. i. 21.   † Prov. x. 7.

An HYMN, Sung after the Sermon.

1 HARK! 'Tis our heav'nly Leader's voice
  From his triumphant feat:
 Midft all the war's tumultuous noife,
  How pow'rful, and how fweet!

2 " Fight on, my faithful band," he cries,
  " Nor fear the mortal blow:
 " Who firft in fuch a warfare dies,
  " Shall fpeedieft victory know.

3 " I have my days of combat known,
  " And in the duft was laid:
 " But thence I mounted to my throne,
  " And glory crowns my head.

4 " That throne, that glory, you fhall fhare;
  " My hands the crown fhall give:
 " And you the fparkling honours wear,
  " While God himfelf fhall live."

5 Lord, 'tis enough! Our bofoms glow
  With courage, and with love:
 Thine hand fhall bear thy foldiers thro',
  And raife their heads above.

6 My foul, while deaths befet me round,
  Erects her ardent eyes;
 And longs, thro' fome illuftrious wound,
  To ruth and feize the prize.

    F I N I S.